DREAMS OF DELPHINE

Rich Shapero

DREAMS OF DELPHINE

a novel

TooFar
MEDIA

HALF MOON BAY, CALIFORNIA

TooFar Media
500 Stone Pine Road, Box 3169
Half Moon Bay, CA 94019

Library of Congress Cataloging-in-Publication Data is available.

ISBN: 978-1-7335259-7-8

Cover artwork by Eugene Von Bruenchenhein
Cover design by Michael Baron Shaw
Artwork copyright © 2009 Rich Shapero
Additional graphics: Sky Shapero and Michael Baron Shaw

Printed and Bound by CPI Group (UK) Ltd, Croydon, CR0 4YY

25 24 23 22   2 3 4 5

1

A pack of water snakes moved as one, combing the surface. Beneath the wriggling ribbons, something pale appeared—pale and round. A flurry of silver bubbles emerged, impatient breath, the snake trails parted like locks of hair, and a face rose, beaded with foam.

Someone was shaking him. When Presden eased open his lids, her face was before him, smiling, eyes wide. He snapped at the strip of bacon under his nose, missed, then snapped again, crunching it, hearing Delphine's giggles.

He hugged her, and she hugged him, and the smoky odor of bacon was drowned by the hair and cheek smells of his twin.

"No breakfast," he reminded her.

"Bacon doesn't count."

They were eight, a hard age, being burdened with school; but this day was a free one. "Hurry," she said.

She was wearing her overalls. Presden found his pants. "Don't forget."

"Right here." She lifted a canvas shopping bag with something heavy inside.

Through the loft's hatch, a scrubbing sound reached them. Dad had eaten, and Mama was cleaning the skillet. Smells of black coffee, biscuits, red-eye gravy.

Delphine sprang for the ladder. "The clock," Presden said.

He reached under his pillow, grabbed a neck thong with a disk-shaped object attached and drew it over his head.

The twins descended quickly.

Mama was in the kitchen with her apron on, and the back door was open. Through it, Presden saw an orange sun above the trees. In the foreground was water—the bayou, blue and silver. At its edge, a flock of egrets glided as if they were swimming.

Delphine left the ladder and ran to Mama. He did the same, and they hugged her waist. She was tall and slender, and when she stooped to return the double embrace, the sun lit the bronze in her bound hair.

"For your zoo," Mama said, handing an empty jar to each. Presden checked the pinholes in the metal lids. His made a wheel, Delphine's a star. He grabbed a biscuit with his free hand and swiped it through the gravy, then he was out the door, headed down the path to the dock with Delphine right behind.

On the dock they stopped by the salt-cured hides. Muskrat, nutria, a mink with white whiskers, head twisted in a snarl. Delphine patted it. Dad was loading traps into the outboard, one-armed, left-handed. His right sleeve was pinned to his shoulder.

He paused, gliding his palm over the water, welcoming them to the day's adventure like a fellow buccaneer. "Don't get lost," he said. "There's a picnic tomorrow." They had one every Sunday on an island where Dad had built a table and shed. Spanish moss draped the trunks, and emerald grass snakes looped from the branches.

The twins approached him together. They were the same height, and both were limber and lanky. They both had Dad's black hair, but Delphine's was blacker. They both had Mama's sweet nature, but Presden's was sweeter.

Dad gave them each a peck, raised his arm and squeezed Presden's shoulder—his only hand, but stronger for that. Mama descended the path with a pot of coffee, and when she reached Dad, she filled his thermos. He cupped Delphine's neck, then he jumped into his boat and pulled the starter rope with his arm, like a pirate drawing his saber from its sheath.

The engine fired to a coughing idle, unspooling blue smoke. Dad reversed the glugging engine and ruddered out into the channel. Then the boat roared and swung forward in a wide loop, leaving a swerving wake with a wriggling tail. Dad lifted his fist to the sky, and the boat disappeared around the Point.

"Bring my snails," Delphine said.

Presden handed her the empty jam jar and stepped

3

behind Dad's game rack, where water-filled jars and cans were cluttered. He picked up a jar of purple periwinkles.

"Let's go."

The twins had their own boat—a pirogue. Dad had felled a cypress and chopped it with an adze. He burnt and chopped it again and again until it was hollow, smooth and slidy inside. They lowered the jars over the gunnel, and Delphine put the shopping bag in the bows. The sound of Dad's boat rumbled away through the swamp.

"Shall we check our clock?" Mama said.

Presden turned and she lifted the dial from his chest.

"Two hours," she said. "That's 10:15. You be back by then."

"'Course," Presden said.

"Let's set the alarm." Mama clicked the switch. Then she turned to Delphine. "You heed the rules."

Delphine nodded.

Mama knelt, hugged each in turn, kissing their cheeks and their noses. Then she returned up the path to the house.

Delphine took her place at the prow, paddle ready. Presden was in the rear, loosing the mooring rope. He grabbed his pole, plunging it deep, feeling the soft bottom. Then they were moving, free of the stubborn world, headed for adventure and breathless surprises. The bayou was an infinite web. Arms of water stretched in every direction, mysterious and inviting.

"Swamp Fox," Delphine cued him.

Presden grabbed his straw hat and put it on. Mama had

4

pinned a white feather to the band. Behind them, the house-on-stilts grew smaller. Mama stood in the doorway, waving.

Forward, the Point appeared. Herons were feeding along its edge. Presden felt the familiar thrill, mingled with dread and the pricking of sight and sound and smell. Frogs and duckweed, crayfish claws, flesh-colored wrigglers in the creeping sludge—

"Is the can in the water?" Delphine said.

He removed the pole, letting the craft drift while he retrieved the can. It was in good shape, not rusted much. The string was unfrayed and firmly knotted to the nail by his elbow. He tossed the can in the water, watched it trawl behind, then returned to his poling.

The lagoon was wider here. The black water lapped against the hull.

"Turtle," she said.

A soft-shelled turtle floated past, a pancake without the syrup.

"And a snake," he said.

Two yards away, a coal-black water snake twitched its head. In the morning, the lagoon was full of them, like worms in the mud rising after a rain. Each dragged its silver ribbon behind, jiggling blithely. Then all at once, the ribbon pulled straight and the snake shot forward like an arrow being fired. Mysterious creatures, but the patterns revealed some of their secrets.

"Gars," Delphine said.

The needle-nosed fish cruised past like toy submarines.

Then the pirogue was rounding the Point, and the house-on-stilts disappeared.

What looked like a small log was floating in the water directly ahead.

Delphine paused her paddling and pointed.

"Okay," Presden whispered.

She resumed her paddling with a stealthy stroke. He pushed the pole gently, guiding the craft silently closer.

The pirogue kept them safe, but there were rules. They were on a two-hour leash. They were to keep their arms inside the hull, except when they were netting or landing their catches. They could dock their craft and travel on foot in only the agreed-upon places. The most important rules were about gators.

Don't go swimming. Watch for gators and keep away. Dad said no gator was going to bite through the wood to get them, but that gave Mama little comfort. So they heeded the rule and kept their distance, except for the small ones. With them, Presden had devised an exciting sport.

Delphine hunched forward. Closer to the floating log they nosed, closer and closer.

A bump on the log moved and an eye opened.

"Now," he murmured.

Delphine drew her paddle out. Presden raised his pole from the water and extended it, touching the scaly back.

Some just sank, but the battlers—like this one—went crazy, arching, snapping its jaws and thrashing its tail.

Delphine squealed. Presden whooped and fell back. They chortled in triumph as the pirogue drifted past.

Presden gripped the gunnel and drew himself up, resting his chin on the wood. Delphine did the same. Together, they breathed in the swampy odors. Through squinting lids, he scanned the surface. The morning sun glazed the water, lighting its patterns: fish bones and chevrons, ranked and rippling; twists of foam, like ghostly breath; bubble scarves bunching and stretching, pulling apart—patterns that held your gaze and wouldn't let go. It might be the wind, sketching and carving, or the crafty movements of creatures beneath. Or the water itself, all nervous and excited, strange thoughts stirring.

"Check the can," Delphine said.

Presden turned and pulled on the string. When he lifted the trawling can and peered inside, there were two little swamp shrimp, a silver minnow and a baby catfish. Delphine was behind him, looking over his shoulder.

"I like the shrimpies," she said, reaching for a jar by her feet.

"We need a new cat," Presden noted.

They had a rotating zoo in the pirogue—crayfish, snails, tadpoles, a musk turtle, a pair of red-eared sliders and more—all in jars Mama had given them. Delphine found their baby catfish and released it back to the bayou. Presden sloshed the new cat in, while Delphine took the lid off an empty. They added the pair of shrimp to their collection.

Presden faced her. "Oysters."

"Oysters," she nodded, crawling forward, grabbing her paddle.

Presden dug his pole in, and the pirogue glided over the glittering water.

They weren't supposed to leave Teredo Lagoon, the pocket of water they called home. But the Island of Rocks wasn't far beyond, and on a recent trip they'd spotted oysters. They didn't know how to land the pirogue or remove the shellfish. That was the challenge.

As the pirogue emerged from the lagoon's mouth, the speckled rocks of the Island appeared. The tide is low, Presden thought. The oysters will be in reach. He imagined the triumph when the prize was in hand, the excitement they'd feel when they pried them open. Oyster, oyster— What was their story?

The rocks loomed larger as they approached. Around the Island, he saw, the water was churning—instead of being flat or sluppy, it had tubes as thick as your leg. The current was rolling over itself. Could they take the pirogue into that?

"Not sure," Presden muttered.

"Keep on," Delphine said. She was paddling hard.

The closer they came, the more dangerous the water looked. The pirogue was bouncing now, and the turning tubes were larger. "Not sure," Presden repeated, alarmed. But he was still poling.

"Look out," Delphine cried.

The pirogue bucked. Its front spiked, its hind end shook. Presden gripped the gunnel, seeing the water curling beneath as the craft heeled. Then it was thumping and squealing against the rocks, throwing him down.

"Did it," she gasped.

As Presden raised himself, he saw Delphine grab the screwdriver they'd poached from Dad's shed and crane over the bow, reaching beneath the water. The pirogue banged and she shrieked. Then she shrieked again and waved her fist in the air. She was holding a wrinkly shell, green with red hairs. She dropped it between them and bent again to pry more oysters loose.

The pirogue lurched and thumped. Presden grabbed his pole.

A blade of rock screeched against the hull. As he watched, a strip of cypress rose from the bow like a carrot being peeled. The pirogue was groaning, tipping—

"Hang on," Presden yelled. He rammed his pole and pushed off.

Delphine jerked back, falling onto her side.

The craft rumbled over the turning tubes, reached flat water and began to glide.

She raised herself, eyes wide. "Got 'em," she said.

They let the pirogue drift on its own while they examined the catch.

There were three oysters. The smallest was the greeny with red hair, another was purple-brown, and the largest was gray with white streaks. Their backs had ridges, and their edges were brittle and flaky. "Open up," Delphine said, shaking one. They were all closed tight. "I want to see—"

9

"At the Story Tree," Presden said.

She met his gaze, considering. "Okay." Delphine put the oyster down. Then her eyes glittered. "Let's swim first," she dared him.

They were beyond the Point, out of anyone's view.

He shook his head.

"I belong in the water," she argued. "I'm water inside, not dirt and rocks."

He scooped his hand over the surface and splashed her, and she splashed him back. They rocked the pirogue with their game until they were soaked. Then, because the sun was getting hot, they washed their arms like raccoons, filled a jar with water and poured it over their heads, as pleased by that as if they'd jumped in.

Delphine put her arm behind her back. "I'm Dad."

"You still have one left," Presden said, "and it's a good one."

She nodded. "Better than most. Let's go to the Story Tree."

They headed back to Teredo Lagoon, entered its reedy mouth and followed a branching channel. They swung twice to the right, crossed a pool tiled with leaves and roped the pirogue to a rotting wharf. Its piers were riddled with teredos. The shipworms had given the lagoon its name, and they were easy to find and creepy to play with.

It was often like that—they had the Story Tree in mind, but something exciting got in the way. They circled a post, pulling woody flakes loose, looking for the gleam and the slime. A teredo's long body was rubbery, and you could see through it. And it had a strange odor, fetid, musky—the smell of rainwater inside an old tire, ripe with wiggle-tails and mold.

"I got one," Delphine exclaimed, wrinkling her nose, pulling the worm out of the rotting timber. It stretched like gum, longer and longer.

"It's as long as your arm," she said.

"No it's not."

To prove she was right, Delphine made him hold the teredo's nose and extend his arm. She drew the worm along it, all the way to his shoulder.

"See," she said. "It's as long as Mr. Stretchy."

"It's Junior Stretchy," he conceded.

She giggled, took the worm's head and brought it toward him.

Presden raised his hand.

The worms were so soft, it was hard to understand how they made their tunnels, but when you looked at the head, the mystery was solved. The teredo's mouth had tiny blades. When Delphine touched the blades to his palm, Presden felt the tickling sensation. "Me too," Delphine said, passing the worm to him and raising her hand. Presden put the teredo's head to the tip of her first finger. Delphine tittered and joggled her shoulders.

She looked at the water beyond the pier. "Let's swim."

Presden irked his brows.

"Put our heads in the water," she said. "Just our heads."

He agreed, so they knelt and dunked together. The wharf was a fine place for that, because the water was swirling, and you could see bubble scarves moving in all directions, like an invisible giant putting on a small shirt.

When they raised their heads, terns were wheeling above them, frantic and white, fluttering and piping.

"Get the oysters," Presden said, lifting the shopping bag from the pirogue.

Delphine put the shellfish in the bag and the screwdriver in her pocket, and they started over the rotted planking. With his free arm, Presden circled her, feinting as if he would bump her into the water. She wrestled free, and they stumbled onto the muddy bank.

A path led through the cypress. The land was boggy and swampy. Danger might be lurking here, so they followed the trail with care, pausing now and again to scout the way. No gators, but they spotted a box turtle barging through the leaves. It had bright red markings on its shell, like the pieces of a puzzle.

They reached a large clearing with a giant cypress at its center.

Presden removed his belt and strapped the shopping bag and its contents to his back. Then he wrapped his arms around the trunk and began scooching toward the lowest limb. Delphine followed. When they reached the limb, they got their butts on it and slid along. Six feet from the trunk was a scoop, where the fibrous bark was soft and loose.

They halted and wiggled their rears, settling into the perch.

Delphine unstrapped the canvas bag from his back, and together they removed the Storybook. It was a double-winged courthouse book for deeds and records. Mama had found it at a yard sale. Presden set the water-stained volume in his lap. Delphine opened the cover with both hands and began turning pages. There were drawings and words on each.

A circle of dancing crayfish. Pelicans carrying their babies. A giant serpent rising from the lagoon, staring straight at you—Delphine drew that on a hot day when she was half-asleep. There was a picture of the house-on-stilts with Dad and Mama in it—they were creatures too and had earned a page of their own.

As the twins learned about the bayou's inhabitants, they made up stories about them and added drawings to the book. An image of Mr. Stretchy reached across two pages; a stick-figure girl held the head, and a stick-figure boy held the tail. On the next page, a swarm of birds fluttered, frantic with curiosity, crazy to know: what do you wish for, what do you want most of all? If you told them, the Wish Terns could make the wish come true. Below them, Presden had drawn the water and its magic patterns.

"Now," Delphine said, taking the large gray oyster from the bag.

She turned it in her fingers, finding the seam where the wrinkled lips met. "There." She handed the screwdriver to him.

It was a struggle, but Presden managed to fit the blade in and pry it open.

"He's fat," Delphine exclaimed.

"Is it alive?" He pushed the lumpy mass with his finger.

"Sure. He's watching us."

Presden pulled the cigar box out of the shopping bag and raised the lid. Delphine turned to a blank page in the Storybook and set the oyster on it. Then she bit her lip and picked a colored pencil from the box.

She drew a wide head with wrinkly lips. Then she added ears and squinty eyes.

"You," she said.

He selected a pencil and made a droopy tongue.

"It's a palace," she said, "and he's duke."

"No," he shook his head, drawing water patterns on either side.

"It's a store and he's boss," Delphine said.

"Nope."

"It's a hash house and he's cook."

Presden found a black pencil. "It's a court and he's judge," he said. "He decides what's right and wrong, who's guilty and who's not. This gentl'man, he's Big Oyster, judge of the Oyster People." He drew a robe on him. Then he began sketching smaller oysters on either side.

Delphine nodded. "The others help him make up his mind."

She focused on the margin, drawing oysters down it.

Presden put expressions on Big Oyster's cronies. One was

mellow, forgiving. Another was dour, contentious. A third was harsh, without mercy. Next he drew a smaller oyster above and to the side.

"Who's that?" Delphine asked.

"Greeny," Presden said. "Give me a red pencil."

"What does he do?"

"Not sure." Presden added red hairs to Greeny and put bubbles above him.

Delphine was penciling the bottom of the page.

"What are those?"

"The Oyster Sisters. They sing." She grinned. "They have a beautiful sound. You're here too," she added a stick figure beside the Sisters, "and there's a mermaid with you." She drew a creature with a fish's tail. "That's me!" She dashed her hand out and pinched him.

Presden shirked and giggled, "Big Oyster can't see mermaids."

"He's seeing one now," Delphine shrieked, tickling his middle.

Just then, the alarm went off. Presden drew a breath, raised the clock on his chest, clicked the switch and the ringing stopped.

Delphine's eyes fixed on his. "Tonight," she said.

He shook his head. "Not till the moon's full."

She set her palm on the open book. They longed to venture out in the darkness, to see the night secrets, when all the creatures hidden during the day would emerge.

The air was warm now. The cicadas were buzzing. Presden

put his hand beside hers, sharing her passion for the stories that would grace the empty pages.

At the shake, Presden rolled over. Delphine stood by his bed with her finger to her lips. She held a glass jar in her hand, filled with lightning bugs.

He peeled the blanket away—he'd gone to bed fully dressed, as they'd planned. She passed him a second sparking lantern and led the way down the ladder. When they reached the back door, she opened it for him. The trilling of tree frogs was like a wall. He took a breath and walked straight into it, feeling the *lurps* like bubbles bursting. Then they were crossing the porch side by side, hurrying down the path to the floating dock, braving the mystery. When they reached the pirogue, he looked up, and it was as if he was dreaming, drifting in a pool of fog between winking constellations.

Dad and Mama would never know. The pirogue would be back before dawn. By then, the fireflies would be dim. Delphine would empty them onto the planks where they would crawl like dying embers, while the two of them snuck through the door, ascended the ladder and returned to their beds.

He held the craft steady and Delphine climbed in, taking her position at the prow. He boarded and clambered aft to untie the rope. She secured her lantern, and with fireflies fore and aft, Presden dug the pole in and pushed off, guiding the pirogue away from the dock over black water.

Frogs were shrilling from every tree, and the bullfrogs were drumming, their groans so deep they sounded like cattle. He heard the hollow splash of a fish, and when he turned he could see the house-on-stilts silhouetted by stars, like an ancient castle, the king and queen still fast asleep as if under a spell.

When the pirogue had rounded the Point, Delphine pulled the flashlight from her pocket and turned it on, flooding the shoreline. The beam surprised two nutria swimming toward them—they paused and plunged. A raccoon on a half-drowned branch was dipping for minnows. It *chirred* and stood, dazzled, covering its eyes with both paws. Delphine laughed and swung the beam, surprising a swarm of life. A flock of ducks quacked and leapt into the night. A snake scribed a hurried ess while nightjars skimmed the surface around it. A screech owl whimpered and a bullfrog lowed, this one so close it might have been in the pirogue.

Presden poled forward, breathless. The craft left a silvery vee and, on either side, the water was patterned with guiding ripples and signaling stars—inviting, luring, as if the ghostly lagoon was aware of their presence.

"I love it," Delphine said.

"It's kind of scary."

If they ran aground and couldn't get free, what would he do? He could make a fire like the ones Dad made, but he didn't have matches. Or a hubcap. A little fire didn't warm you, but it kept you company.

Moths fluttered in the flashlight beam, spinning down

to the water, whirring in circles. A fish rose and snapped at them.

"Like to pole for a while?"

Delphine laughed. "Want a turn in front?"

But neither moved.

An arm of the lagoon opened on the right, an arm Presden didn't recall. He steered the pirogue into it.

Delphine grew still, as if she too was struggling to remember where they were.

The bayou was silent now. Presden heard the trickle of water running off the pole.

The fireflies in the forward lantern began to blink, all together. Delphine looked at him, puzzled, wondering what it meant. And then, as Presden watched, her eyes grew wider and her lips trembled, as if she was sensing something he couldn't see or hear.

"What is it?" he whispered.

The fireflies in the rear lantern joined the alarm, blinking too. Warning them.

"Don't worry," Presden said. But his heart was pounding.

It was as if they had passed through an invisible curtain—joy on one side, fear on the other. Delphine felt the danger and so did he. It was all around them, and inside them too, drowning everything.

All at once, more than anything, Presden wanted to go home. He wished they hadn't snuck out of the house-on-stilts, wished they hadn't pushed away from the dock, wished their fancies hadn't drawn them into the darkness.

Delphine looked pale and stricken, lips taut, as if she was in physical pain. Her eyes were sorry, so sorry— Presden searched for a joke or an adage, something to distract her, to calm them both.

And then—

The water beside him cleaved and erupted in a way he had never seen. A dark land rose, with cascades streaming from ridges and terraces, swelling impossibly. And a terrible smell, smothering close—

Presden could see the crest of its back, spiked and plated, broader than the pirogue itself. How could an animal be that big? Where was its head, its jaw, its tail?

They were tipping. Presden dug with his pole, the rilling prongs, the shifting scales and wrinkled skin filling his sight—an ancient nightmare, a horror from long ago.

The craft lurched onto its side as if flipped by a giant hand. The menagerie clattered, all their collected cans and jars with creatures in them, and as their brave ship capsized, he saw Delphine's face. She was startled, confused, but no longer frightened. She must not have seen what he'd seen— the size and the darkness of it. Her mouth opened, about to speak. No words, just a gasp as they struck the water.

Presden kicked and thrashed his arms, fighting his soaked clothes, trying to see her, struggling to get to the other side of the craft. Not a gasp of fear, he thought. She sounded perplexed. Did she think he'd made a mistake with the pole?

The gator bumped them by accident—that's what he hoped. But they were close to it now, very close. He could feel the beast churning the water. He imagined its giant teeth finding him, piercing him, pulling him under.

His hands gripped wood. The inverted pirogue— He inched around it. Where was his twin? What was she thinking? He couldn't shout or cry out. The black water tugged, but he kept his silence, hiding his terror to keep the monster from knowing.

Then the wood was torn from his grasp. The pirogue bounced and cracked, lashed by an enormous tail. Something rough and alive dug into Presden's chest. The water around him humped and foamed, and the streaming monster rose before him, opening its jaws against the sky. Moonlit fangs, periscope eyes—

Swim, he urged his sister. *Swim to the bank, grab on to a tree.*

Delphine— He couldn't see her or hear her.

The sky was vacant now. The monster was sinking back under. Through the water's shuddering curls, a lightning bolt of white belly flashed, then the gator was twisting, spiraling away, a vee-wake and a chain of black bubbles dragging behind.

Then darkness. Darkness and silence.

The water grew calm.

Presden scrabbled up onto the shell of the overturned pirogue.

A sharp pain in his chest. The pole floated beside, bitten in half.

There was a smear of blood on the hull near the prow.

He lay there, guarding his breath, fearful the gator, even at a distance, might hear the pounding of his heart in the hollowed-out craft. It was a desolate sound, stark and forlorn, and it echoed with a terrible suspicion. There had been two hearts, but there was only one now.

Presden raised his head and called her name. And then, unable to stop, he kept on calling. He could no longer feel her near or far; neither did he have any sense of where she might be, or how his voice might reach her. But the name belonged to his sister, and the sound of it kept her present as long as it was in his throat and ears.

After a while, he heard the frogs and an owl hooting. The dark swamp fell back into its many diversions, its unconcerned life; and Presden had nothing to do but feel the throbbing of the wound in his chest while he waited for dawn, the growl of the motorboat, and the sound of his parents shouting, searching the bayou for them.

Beneath the sheets in the loft, Presden felt the black water watching him. Dad fed him pills and changed the bandages on his chest, but the pain didn't fade. It spread down his middle, into his legs. It was only relieved by fits of tears and hysterics. The lagoon was a fearful place now, a place he no longer understood.

Dad drove him to Aunt Lenora's, and staying with her helped him to heal. But when he returned, the Mama he knew and depended on had vanished. The woman in her place was sickened by grief and needed medicine of her own at all hours. When she wasn't weeping, she was crouched on the stoop, treating herself from a cracked teacup.

It took a neighbor and a truant officer to get him to school. Classwork, the playground and new faces calmed him some. Delphine was with him from time to time. She would visit the loft and sit beside him, and the two would talk. He'd share his sadness, and he'd feel better; but then she'd leave, and the dread would be worse than ever. One night, the Gator came with her. It hunkered behind her, watching them both.

The food Mama prepared tasted different now. He recoiled from her touch and the smell of her breath. Dad went trapping for longer and longer stretches. One day he stopped coming home.

Mama's drinking grew worse. When Presden left for school in the morning, he put her out of his mind. But at the end of the day, she was there waiting, morose, often senseless. Then a letter came from Dad's cousin, saying a stroke had ended his life. Presden sat on the vacant dock, imagining Dad's boat moored there, and he cried and cried. The pirate was gone, and so was he. The boy who loved his watery home would never return.

Then a blessing reached him from an unexpected quarter. The discipline of facts, of numbers and analysis. He had imagined the true Presden was lost. What a surprise it was to find him in geometry, in chemistry and math. As unlikely as it seemed, those subjects had the surety of firm ground. It was there the mind found an answer to the dangers of a disordered world.

He had never cared for school, but it was school that saved him. The magical patterns that seduced the child's mind were, he saw, untrustworthy, unpredictable. And what had seemed oppressive, rigid and boring, was a source of strength, a stormproof shelter. About this time, he invented a game. It settled his sleep and kept the dreams of gators away. With the game, Delphine's visits ceased.

Presden found he liked learning. His teachers said he was smart. And the security he found in his new passion took the pressure off Mama. She understood nothing of the subjects that drew him, but that bolstered her confidence. Presden had found his own footing and needed little from her.

He learned drafting in high school and found a faculty mentor, and on graduation he was admitted to a highly ranked technical institute in New York, on the Hudson River, with a scholarship that covered most of the costs. So with Mama's good wishes, he packed his things. On the day he left, she told him that she didn't want him to be afraid. "Don't let anything frighten you or throw you off course," because if that happened, it would mean "the gator had taken you both." After so many unsteady years, Presden saw resolve in his mother's eyes, and hope.

At college, he did his best to care for her, securing a part-time job, sending her what funds he could and returning home when breaks permitted. Thankfully she found work at an eatery in town and her drinking abated.

With encouragement from one of his professors, Presden applied for and was admitted to the institute's doctoral program. He was drawn to structural engineering, and as it happened, the school was a recognized leader in coastal hydrology, a field that he found compelling. To understand water's power, to know how to control it—the idea inspired him.

He graduated at the top of his class and took a job with an engineering firm headquartered in Virginia, designing projects up and down the coast. Land and sea, the negotiable border— All of his work was at the water's edge. Seawalls, levees, submarine foundations— He had the know-how to stop the water, to hold it back, to control and contain it. For Presden this was a kind of reprisal. Perhaps it was a desire to deny his wound, or some vestige of Storybook theatrics, but he viewed his life now as a morality play. When the forms were removed, and he saw the structures he'd designed withstanding the waves and wildness, he felt a triumph that had nothing to do with timelines or expenses.

He had been at the firm for two years, and he had a routine. He would rise before daybreak and run along the shore, no matter the weather. The strain in his legs, the deep breathing, the feeling of expansion in his chest— The exertion braced him for battle. That was how he met Merle. They were both twenty-seven.

It was spring, and he had seen her three days in a row, sitting on a bench facing the dawn, watching the glow spread over the sea. She wore suede boots and a coral watch cap, alert but expressionless with a book in her lap.

He had smiled at her the first day, and he slowed to greet her on the second. Her cheeks were freckled, her eyes pale green, as if she'd lived in the sun and never known darkness. Presden told himself he would speak to her if she was there a third time, and he did just that. He sat down on the bench, introduced himself and asked her name.

"Merle," she said.

"What are you reading, Merle?"

She looked at the book as if she'd forgotten it. "It's about a young sculptor and his love affair with a creature that lives in the sea."

Only now did she eye him directly. Tentative, cautious— But her reserve had nothing to do with mistrusting the world. She was just a bit shy. Years later, she would tell him she too had counted to three, and if he hadn't sat down on that third day, there wouldn't have been a fourth.

Her hair was sandy, fishhooked beneath her chin, and she nosed the air when she spoke, as if assessing the impact of her words. She had a depth that felt familiar, absent the peril and tragedy. Her English was perfect, so he assumed incorrectly that she was American. Merle was Dutch. She'd grown up near Amsterdam, learned English in school there, attended college in Virginia and had worked in D.C. for five years.

"For someone like me," Presden told her, "Holland is Valhalla. I'm an engineer, a hydrologist. Where the sea meets the land—"

Her smile stopped him. "That's why you're jogging here."

Presden didn't reply.

She looked past him, at the incoming tide.

"I suppose it is," he said. "I'm from Louisiana."

"You have dikes there."

"We do. We call them levees."

"The water's in my blood," Merle said.

Presden shifted beside her, following her gaze, seeing beyond the surf to the silver chevrons, the ranks of winding snakes lit by the dawn.

"I was born in a lagoon," he said, "in a house on stilts, a dozen feet below sea level."

"Water brings life," Merle said.

And water takes it away, he thought. But he held his tongue. Her understanding is deeper than mine, he thought. Or her safety had never been challenged. One or the other. Or perhaps it was both.

She regarded him. "What is it?"

"I had a sister."

"Had?"

He sighed. "You remind me of her."

When Merle asked for more, at first he declined. It was her courage and candor that freed his tongue. She was sharing her awkwardness as a child, out of place with others, lonely and helpless. In the water she found her strength. "Swimming makes me feel alive," Merle said.

In a flash he recalled his boyhood joy, and he told her about splashing and dunking, the floating zoo and the thrill of exploring Teredo Lagoon.

They called in late for work and talked for two hours.

Merle was born on the Holland coast, but a change in her father's employment had driven them inland. She swam for recreation at first, then competitively in college. She had a younger sister back home, Merle said, "with the confidence and social awareness I lack." Then she asked again, and this time he answered.

He told her about the daylight forays, and the plan they hatched to see the bayou at night. Then he told her how he'd lost his sister, and what had happened to Dad and Mama. As he spoke, he felt his sadness surfacing. He struggled to keep it down, but he wasn't able. *It's too much for her*, he thought. Too much damage, too much grief. But she didn't recoil. Merle put her hand on his.

The baffle of clouds, the sidelong rays— When he lifted his head and peered into her eyes, Presden saw golden patterns. Circlets and bangles, rippling lines scribed by dawn's pencils. He was silent. She said not a word. But it seemed that an unconscious tension, a rigor inside him, was finally relaxing.

When he said he wanted to see her again, she invited him to go out in a dinghy. Was she daring him? Did she think she could mend him? Did she mean to show him she wasn't afraid?

Merle made the arrangements, and when they shoved off, she insisted on rowing to show him her skill.

"Does it bother you, not seeing where you're going?"

"I always know where I'm going," Merle replied.

They met for dinner twice, and at the end of the week she asked him to go swimming with her.

"These days," he said drily, "I'm not in the water much."

"You might enjoy it," she deadpanned back. "Being half-naked with me."

She understood the morality play, he thought. Presden Against the Sea. She was calling the play a farce, dragging him off the stage.

"Don't tell me you can't swim," she laughed.

That night, they were intimate. Three weeks later, they were living together.

Two weeks after that, Presden heard from the parish police that Mama had died in her sleep. He scheduled a return trip to bury her, and Merle offered to go with him. He accepted her offer, and then he thought better. He had told her about his ill-fated beginnings—that was enough.

The day before departing, he rented a dory and they launched it in a quiet cove. "There will be pain and sorrow," Merle said. "Let's do what we can to be happy." And Presden agreed.

They joked about rowing and this time he insisted. But as they crossed the water, he felt the distance growing between them. Their words were few. She was disappointed he'd chosen to face his mother's death alone. Disappointed and hurt. She had no way of understanding the guilt, the fear and self-doubt, his return trip would stir. He barely understood it himself. *I just want to protect you*, he thought.

Merle reached for a bright-colored beach bag. He'd brought sandwiches, chips, crackers and cheese. She'd brought lotion, matches and pot. She removed the lotion and rubbed it onto her arms and legs. Then she rolled a joint and lit it. Presden feathered the oars and pulled them out. She drew on the joint and passed it to him without a word. He took a deep draft. Merle removed her floppy straw hat and peered at him. The boat was drifting across the mirror surface.

"I'm not feeling anything," he murmured, setting the joint on the thwart.

To judge from her blank expression, neither was she. Merle angled her head at the sun. Then she put her hands behind her and untied her bikini top. As he watched, she straightened her arms and curled over the gunnel, plunging in.

For a moment, she was gone. There was only the portal and a circle of foam around it. Then she surfaced, laughing and shrieking, gasping and throwing her hair back. Merle treaded the thick water, thighs scissoring, strong as a horse. She met his gaze and motioned to him.

Presden stared at the flashing mirror, remembering. Then he unbuttoned his shirt, pulled off his trunks and dove in.

The water wasn't as cold as he'd thought, and there was no discernible current. It was like a bracing bath. He laughed and leaned forward, stroking and kicking his way to her. She faced him and reached her arms out, and he slid between them like a boat drifting into its slip, silent, welcomed, glad to be home.

"We're lucky," she said, "aren't we."

"We are," he agreed.

Nothing fazed her, nothing dissuaded her; and with all that steadiness came a boundless affection. As their lips met, his mind was a racket of thoughts, things he wanted to say for the first time out loud.

"So lucky," she said.

He grasped her arm, feeling her biceps blindly, loving her muscularity. She wrapped her leg around him and he felt her thigh as the kiss resumed, going deeper. She was strong, an athlete at home in the water. Unreasoning fears, buried deep and unspoken— The things that threatened two kids in Teredo Lagoon were nothing to Merle.

He raised his hands, using his thumbs to clear the water from her lashes. Her eyes were beaming.

Presden shook his head. "Am I going to spend the rest of my life with you?"

"Are you?" she answered, as if she had fallen utterly, and the decision was up to him.

A tear-shaped groove descended from the tail of Merle's right eye, from a bike accident when she was a child. Presden put his finger on it and kissed it. To return the care, she touched the scar on his chest, the wound he carried from that fateful night. She kissed it to honor his sister's memory and the love he still held so close to his heart.

They treaded water, pressing together. Then Presden's arms fell, and the water flowed between them, colder and darker.

"You're thinking about your mother," she said.

He nodded without speaking. Then, like the last two mourners turning from an open grave, they paddled back to the dory.

By the time they climbed over the gunnels, they were shivering.

"Why," Presden asked, turning to face her. "Why would someone who has so little to grieve be drawn to someone who has so much?"

Merle absorbed the question as she toweled herself off. She bent over the gunnel and squeezed the water out of her hair. Then she spoke.

"I feel raw and alive with you. It frightens me. But you've woken me up. I don't want to fall back asleep."

He remembered the morning they'd met.

"I knew," she said. "I just knew."

Presden found her shirt. He opened it, and she slid her arms in. He mis-buttoned the front, but she let it be.

"I want you to come to Holland," she said, "to meet my parents and my sister. 'The mystery man.'" She laughed. "They thought it would never happen." And then, "Family is important to me. I want one of my own some day."

"I think I'd be a good father."

"Do you?"

He'd never thought about it, but what he'd said pleased her, and it pleased him too. Presden nodded. "I do."

The boat swayed as if it was listening and shared their amity. The dory seemed suddenly larger to Presden, large enough to be loaded with supplies for a journey, supplies that would last days, weeks, even years. They would be like creatures from fable. A brace of winged whales would jockey the hull, flocks of seabirds would swirl like waterspouts, charting the way.

He could see the future in Merle's eyes. All his days and years lay ahead, hopeful and changed.

2

Presden was down on his knees before a tomato trellis. He dozed the soil with his hands, filling in holes, securing the posts. On one side of the plot they'd leveled, there were piles of troweled-up weeds. On the other were ranks of pots filled with mulch.

They had talked of having a garden in this spot the day they'd first seen the home. And they'd talked about it every spring since. There had been three, but it felt like more. That morning the simple labors had focused his senses and settled his mind for the visit to come.

The back door creaked open.

Merle ascended the stone steps with a pastry in her hand.

Presden rocked back on his heels and opened his mouth. She put the tart between his teeth, turning to admire his work. "I'd be happy to live here the rest of my life," Merle said the day they moved in, and the garden was, in its small way, a fulfillment of that desire.

She grinned to herself. "It's happening," she murmured. "It really is."

Presden laughed as he rose. Her reaction seemed outsized for tomatoes.

They descended the steps to the bricked patio, where he pulled on his knee boots.

"You're nervous," she said.

"A little."

"He'll be pleased with what he sees," Merle said.

He nodded.

"You've spoken before," she said.

"Only in passing. He's quite a character."

Merle checked the time. "Eight sharp. Did he say how long— When you're done, I have a few things we need to talk over."

"You're not going to work?"

"Not till noon." She grinned again.

What is it? he wondered. She was like a child with a secret.

As they entered the kitchen, the front doorbell rang.

They stepped down the hall together.

When Presden opened the door, the Count's head was bowed. He was winding an antique pocket watch, his cocked elbows flaring a dark cape behind him. In the drive was the gray unmarked car with his driver in it.

The Count raised his head, smiled at Merle, winked at

Presden and crossed the threshold, removing his black fedora. Like Presden, he was wearing twill trousers and rubber knee boots.

"Would you like to sit down?" Presden asked. "We have tea or—"

"I wish there was time." The Count led the way down the hall, glancing into the front room as he passed. "This place is heaven, heaven on earth."

He paused in the kitchen, smoothed his silver mustache with his finger and turned. "Let's get to it."

Presden nodded and opened the back door. The Count's eyes met Merle's. "Forgive me for being rushed."

They started up the stone steps that ascended the dike's land side, Presden in front and the Count behind. Below the crest, the hood of the barbecue lay in their way, thrown free in the night. Presden lifted it and set it back on the grill.

He reached the top and paused there, scanning the sea. The Count stepped beside him. The water was calm, a million scoops of light caught in the dimpled surface. The dock was visible, along with an old motorboat with a mahogany deck, moored to a pier.

The Count inhaled deeply. A show of humanity, Presden thought. Or perhaps, like himself, the man felt braced by the crisp sea air. Presden turned and the Count turned with him. Inland, to the east, the sun was rising above a ridge of dark dunes. Long rays reached toward the dike, touching the Droomwater roofs.

Presden motioned, and the two started along the path

that followed the crest, the warmth of the sun on their cheeks, the sound of the sea in their ears. The dike was a long, peaked hill, and the village of Droomwater lined its land side, fifty-four homes in an undulating row, planted like teeth on an open zipper. The front doors faced the road, but at the rear, most had lofts with windows and a view of the sea. Their home, his and Merle's, was like the others, two stories high, narrow and deep, with a steeply pitched roof, wooden siding and a gable facade. The walls were pale blue, a shade Merle had picked. It went well with the brick-colored roof.

On the sea side, the dike was tiled with gray basalt, and as the sun struck them, the tiles flashed like fish scales. Ferns rooted among them waved in the breeze, like a script from the past, centuries old. He had found his way, Presden thought, from the youth and warmth of the Gulf, to the cooler eastern seaboard, to this oldest and coldest place in the North Atlantic. Wrack lines wandered the beach. Drops from rain a week past pocked the sand. Far out to sea, lanes of froth furrowed the surface.

"It's a page from the past," the Count said, admiring the cottages.

"There's respect for that here," Presden said.

The well-kept planters, the tidy homes—the residents' care showed regard for eight centuries of tradition. Droomwater still had the charm of a medieval fishing village.

As they rounded a bend, a painter appeared facing the water, his easel propped beside the path. The man raised his

brush and dabbed the canvas. A flock of terns piped and dart-
ed, crowding a patch of air beyond the surf line. Twenty feet
farther along the path, someone had left a perch to die. Its
feathery gills twitched in the wind.

"The men who built this," the Count said, "were defying
the will of the sea. Do you think they had any idea what that
meant?"

"They lacked the technical understanding," Presden said.

"Like all our dikes, the plants that mortar those tiles are
non-natives," the Count went on. "One can't help but wonder
what wild blossoms, swept by wind and watered by fog, might
have found a home here."

Presden didn't know how to respond. Did the Count really want to talk about flowers?

"We live in an era of new ideas," the Count said. "An odd
perspective for someone like me." He laughed. "But even I
can be modern. Today we revere the will of nature, do we not?
Today we question the wisdom of our designs. We say: they
have as much right—these seeds that appear from nowhere
and plant themselves without the help of a human hand. And
they have as much spirit—maybe more. They surprise the
senses with their colors and scents. They have the courage of
life, a life of their own."

Presden inclined his head. "Many in the village agree
with you. The people who chose these plants thought only of
stabilizing the soil." Factual, respectful. "Native flora could
do the job, if the Board wanted to fund a replanting."

The Count laughed and bucked his chin, as if he enjoyed the banter. Perhaps, Presden thought, his eccentric habits eased the burden of authority.

The crest tended up, and as they mounted the path, Presden saw the Widow Muldar headed toward them with her staby hound. She treated the path as her own, patrolling it like a sentry, gimping back and forth, clothed like a man, supporting her weak leg with a staff or a patched umbrella. The hound, black and white with copper eyes, was in front, straining at his leash.

"Good morning," Presden greeted her. "This is the Count of—"

"I know who he is."

Her voice was sharp as a knife. The tang of cider was on her breath.

"I've been with the workers," she told the Count. "I give them buttered bread in the morning." She squinted and mashed her jaws.

The Count bowed his head, thanking her.

"My man helped with repairs all his life." The Widow looked at the sea. "We weathered many hardships."

She never stopped talking about her husband. Presden met the man before he died. He was soft-spoken and tolerant, accepting her fractious nature without complaint. The Widow's clothing was dowdy and badly worn, but she kept her ring polished. The stone it held might have been cut the day before.

The Count bid her good day, and they continued along

38

the path. A hundred feet farther, it turned again and the breach came into view. The dike was narrower here, and lower; and instead of a rounded crown, the crest was crumbling, chopped and sunken, with a cage of guardrails around it. Workers jostled within.

Presden pointed at a weathered cottage, just past the breach. "That's hers."

"It doesn't look steady," the Count said.

A dozen of the villagers' homes were leaning, some inland, some toward the sea. The Widow's was worst—fifteen degrees out of true, the landward foundations sinking into the peat. Behind it, the church tower loomed. Its dark brick had been laid during the Middle Ages. The belfry had eight sides with a keyhole in each.

"Do your neighbors have any idea?" the Count asked.

Presden shook his head. "I didn't want to alarm them. I've asked the workers to keep things to themselves until we have more information."

Droomwater was Presden's home, and his job was to protect it. An unlikely chain of events. He had come to Holland with Merle before they were married, to meet her family and see the country. On a referral from a Stateside colleague, he visited an engineering firm in Amsterdam. He was impressed with their projects and they were impressed with his. Merle was ecstatic when they offered him a job. They were married in her homeland, she found work and they rented in town. Eighteen months later they bought the house on the dike. When the breach first appeared, the Water Board—over which the Count presided—needed a structural engineer, and they thought he was a logical choice.

Initially it seemed the problems were minor, but tests had brought more serious things to light. A couple of years before, waves from a winter storm had overtopped the dike, and patches of the land side's clay layer had washed away. By spring, there were further signs of erosion, and when summer came, the peat cracked in the heat. Another wet winter and the cracks expanded. Near the Widow's home, the crown began to collapse. After Presden inspected the breach, he had probes inserted the length of the dike. With every report, the data looked worse. There was work yet to do, but it was already apparent—Droomwater was more threatened than anyone thought. None of the residents were yet aware. Not even Merle.

As they approached the breach, the Count saw the pumping dredge in the water beyond the surf. From its deck a thick gray tube rose, extending through the waves and up the slope. Two men held the tube's nozzle over the breach, and it twitched like an elephant's trunk as sand from the sea floor moved inside it. Others knelt in the black muck, lowering sandbags, while haulers ascended the land side with bags on their backs.

"What's the dredge telling you?" the Count asked.

"I wanted to see how much sand the breach would swallow."

"And?"

"It's taking everything we can pump into it."

Seeing the Count's troubled look, Presden made his request. "I need some budget leeway."

"For what?"

"Infrared aerial photos. A thermographic analysis of the dike, end to end."

"Fine," the Count nodded. He was gazing beyond the breach. "What's the risk?"

"If the dike gives way here, the sea will flood homes on either side. It might reach the church. A lot of property could be damaged."

"Not life-threatening?"

"No, not likely," Presden said. "But the prospect of further collapses might make evacuation necessary. The peat is waterlogged forty feet down. If it goes, it could tear like soggy bread. I've got monitors on it, but there's just no telling."

The village was calm. The residents were accustomed to seeing work on the dike and assumed the breach would be fixed. That was the Water Board's job.

"Ho," Presden shouted, stepping forward.

Those down in the collapse halted their work and climbed out.

Presden waved to a man on the dredge. The pump motor died, and the tube lay still.

"The Count," Presden introduced the big man. "He'd like to see for himself."

Those around the breach made way.

"You'll need this," a grimy woman said.

She handed the Count a chest harness. Presden took one too. When they'd donned them, the woman clipped them to cables. The peat was black. It crumbled beneath Presden's boots, wafered and weak.

"Watch yourself," the grimy woman warned the Count.

"Where do I put my feet?"

The pockets were large enough to swallow him whole.

"Follow me," Presden told the Count.

"The dredge can't keep up," a nozzle man said. "As fast as the slumps fill, new ones appear."

Presden set his foot on a ledge. Beneath him, cracks rayed in every direction. The Count shuddered and growled.

Suddenly the ledge beneath Presden's boot vanished.

He dropped, falling his own length before the cable caught him. A gasp choked him, his trembling hands clawed the peat. Above, the grimy woman scowled, holding his weight with the winch.

"Good lord." The Count shook his head.

"You okay?" the nozzle man barked.

Presden's heart was chugging. The peat by his nose was as mushy as boiled grits. "Get me out of here."

The group crowded the winch and raised him back up.

With one arm, Presden steadied himself on the cable; the other circled the shin of the grimy woman. The winch lifted him until he could set his boot on the tumbled rim. The Count snagged his trunk and pulled him to safety.

"I've seen enough," he said.

The two men slogged through the peat to the guardrail. Presden turned, breathed a sigh of thanks to the team and passed through. And they started back along the crest.

Presden was thinking of Merle, chastening himself. Why hadn't he told her? She'd been so radiant recently, so fond and warm. It was the time of year, the promise of spring— He'd continued to hope the breach could be sealed and the trouble settled quickly. There seemed no reason to frighten her.

At the bend in the path, the Count halted.

"The dike's beyond patching, isn't it. It will have to be rebuilt."

"The advanced diagnostics will tell us," Presden said.

"How long?"

"A few days."

"I have confidence in you," the Count said. "I'm glad you're in charge."

His words were some kind of preamble.

"I'll wait to see your conclusions," the Count continued. "But there is a belief among some on the Board, myself included, that we shouldn't lose sight of the longer perspective. Before we tend to Droomwater's need, we have to answer a deeper question." He gazed at the sea.

"Which is?"

"What is the proper province of man?"

The Count's language seemed laughably abstract.

"I'm sorry the news is so—"

The Count turned. His irritation stopped Presden's words.

"If we give way here at Droomwater," the Count said, "and allow the ocean to make its way inland, as it has been trying to do for centuries, the pressure on dikes up and down the coast would be reduced. Correct?"

Presden was stunned, too stunned to respond.

"That would secure other villages, would it not?"

The wind rose. The Count's cape flapped.

Presden was awash with speculations. Was there pressure from a neighboring town? Some political point at stake, or somebody's money? How far had the Water Board gone toward condemning the village? Were they already assessing their homes?

What did they want of him? He could wrestle with the technical issues—the strength of rip tides, the integrity of the dike's foundation—but the Board's motivations were beyond his view.

"We'll evaluate your suggestions for repairing the dike," the Count assured him, "but I want you to expand your scope. And it's clear, that has to happen quickly." Stern, but not cross; official, but not officious. "Along with the rebuild alternatives, I want you to consider whether it might be wiser to give Droomwater back to the sea."

The directive echoed in Presden's head.

"I live here," he said, knowing, even as he objected, that there was a deeper reason the task was unwelcome.

Through Merle, he'd struck an uneasy peace with water. But he made his living fighting the sea, keeping it back; predicting its moods, its storms and surges; defending against its raging incursions. That was his craft, his skill, his talent—

The Count was regarding him.

"What kinds of creatures swam here," the big man wondered, "in eons past?"

"In the Paleozoic, there were crinoids, trilobites, fenestellids; fish and amphibians."

"It's hard to believe it was all underwater."

The Count folded his cape over his knees. Presden closed the rear door of the gray sedan. As it backed down the drive, he watched Merle out of the corner of his eye. She stood by the front entrance unsuspecting. He'd balked at sharing bad news about the breach, and the assignment the Count had just given him made things so much worse. Presden steeled himself and stepped toward her.

Merle raised her hand. She was gazing over his shoulder now, hailing someone behind him. Presden saw a young couple approaching, the woman cheery, the man looking earnest and respectful, holding a platter covered with see-through wrap.

"Good morning," Presden said with an inquiring tone.

"We're next door," the young woman explained. "We just moved in. We wanted to introduce ourselves." She was small and blond and wore a ripped t-shirt.

"We brought you a sea trout," the man said. His orange hair stood up as if he'd taken an electric jolt. He had a stud in his ear.

"Come in, please." Merle motioned them over the threshold.

The couple entered, and Merle led the way down the hall. Presden followed. When they reached the kitchen, the young man set the platter on the table.

"Fonelle," the blond patted her sternum. "This is Jan, my fiancé." She flipped his earlobe to see the stud wink. Jan's face flushed, and they laughed at each other. "It's ready to bake," Fonelle said, turning back to the fish. "Jan caught him. I dressed him up."

"*Wat aardig*," Merle said. "He'll be our guest of honor tonight."

The fish was gape-mouthed, wrapped with baking string and surrounded by lemon slices. In the light from the window, its silver skin glittered.

"We met Mrs. Muldar yesterday," Fonelle told them.

"'The Widow,'" Merle said. "That's what she prefers."

"We brought her a snapper. She showed us the break in the dike."

Merle tapped her toe. "You know Presden is—"

"We've heard." Jan faced him. "Nothing serious, I hope."

"The old dikes need tending," Merle said.

Presden added a reassuring nod. How long would the couple stay? He dreaded the conversation he would have with Merle, but he was ready to have it.

"I teach at the school in Beverwijk," Fonelle said. "Jan is a programmer. He works in the city, but every spare hour he's out in our boat. Have you seen—"

46

"It's a beauty," Presden said.

"I want a garden with peas and hydrangeas," Fonelle told them.

"I can help you with that," Merle said, "and the Widow can too. She's Droomwater's master gardener."

Presden felt his wife's impatience. She was usually so adept with guests.

"Are we making you late?" Fonelle put her hand on Merle's wrist. "You seem like wonderful people. Well—" Fonelle nodded to Jan.

"I proposed the day we moved in," he shared. "We're going to be married in your church this fall."

Fonelle blushed and pulled on his arm. "We'll let ourselves out."

As the young couple stepped down the hall, Merle put the fish in the fridge.

That the dike was unstable, Presden knew, would rattle her. She'd be upset he hadn't shared that earlier. He would ask her forgiveness. Then he'd explain the assignment the Count had given him, and what, if the worst came to pass, might happen to their home. The future was uncertain. It would be hard for them both. He would need her support and her counsel.

Presden started gently. "The work I've been doing—"

Merle sighed as the front door closed, then she laughed and turned.

"What do you think of 'Jovis,'" she said, "for a man's name. It's heavenly, and it's Dutch. Is it too pretentious?"

Presden cocked his head, confused.

"It's strong," she said, "but it's carefree too."

"What are you telling me?"

"I've missed two periods." Merle reached for him. "I'm feeling queasy and strange. Hold me." She lolled her head, acting frail.

Presden embraced her. "How—"

"You must have breached my dike." She laughed.

He had known a moment like this would come.

"I have an appointment with an obstetrician," Merle said.

"When?"

"Tuesday."

Sooner or later, it would come. And he imagined he'd be prepared for it. She was brimming with celebration. He wanted to join in.

"If it's real," Merle said, "I'm going to take time off. Three months, maybe more. The truth is— I've been thinking about quitting. Things have been going so well for us."

Presden didn't reply.

"Would you be okay with that? If I devoted myself to being a mom?"

Presden was shirking inside. Was it the dike and his sense of hazard? Or that the child was accidental? It was something they were going to plan.

"I've been so emotional," Merle confessed. "I think my chemistry's changing." She drew back. Her eyes fixed on him. He could feel her excitement and gladness—her hopes about how he'd react.

"It's happened because we love each other," she said.

He heard her heart in her voice, which made his reaction all the more troubling. He didn't understand it.

"If you're pregnant," he said, "we'll call it good fortune. I'm ready."

The words were right, but his tone wasn't. He sounded reluctant, uncertain.

Merle's head ticked, there was tension in her frame. She was watching him like a shorebird watches a crab.

He wanted to reassure her. Things would turn out. But before he could speak, he saw the concern in her eyes.

After all the trust they'd built up together over the years— Something was wrong, and Merle was wondering what and why.

Presden was dreaming. In his dream he felt pressure and urgency—things had to be decided, but there wasn't much time. He was seated in his office in Amsterdam with computer screens circling him. A map was displayed on each, and he was trying to make sense of them. His hands pulled tables and diagrams from folders, tapped keyboards and paged through reports, moving of their own accord. Over the tops of the screens, he could see, through the windows, the converted warehouses and breweries across the canal—offices like his, but the lights were off.

It was late. He'd been here for days, sleepless and starved, wearing only his shorts. Merle lay in bed at home, waiting for his results. The Count and the Water Board had moved in with her and were waiting there too.

He was drowning in data: images of coastlines, soundings and tides, levels expressed in means and extremes, stats about the dike's defenses dozens of miles north and south. New variables poured in, predictions circled the future but couldn't catch it, equations changed on their own— And then, all at once, the answer surfaced, flawless and indisputable.

A sudden racket—rain splattered the windows. As Presden looked up, the mist beyond the pane tumbled against it and a large comber broke through, dousing his screens, covering his desk. He hurled himself back, watching the froth dissolve; and with it, his reports and charts and piles of folders, and the perfect solution he'd found.

The intercom buzzed. Building security.

Presden touched the red button. "What is it?"

"Your mother's in the lobby," the guard said. "She's waiting to see you."

Presden shook his head. "My mother died years ago."

"She says she's your Mama."

The Widow, Presden thought. She'd come on behalf of the angry villagers.

He rode the elevator down three floors to the lobby. The security kiosk was empty. The guard was gone, but he'd left his thermos. The top was off, and steam rose from its mouth; and with the steam, came the odor of coffee and biscuits and red-eye gravy.

In the waiting area, a woman was seated. She was reading an old newspaper, yellow and brittle with age. Her face was hidden, but as Presden approached, she folded the paper and stood.

A jolt went through him. Mama, he thought.

He froze, looking away, his despair returning. The liquor, the grimness, her endless stupor— How could she be so distant, so unreachable?

"My boy," Mama said.

Her voice was warm and knowing. When he turned to look, she smiled.

Her regal bearing had returned. Her bronze hair glinted in the lamplight. This was the old Mama, he realized. The Mama he knew and loved.

She reached her arms out, eyes bright; and when he stepped forward, her embrace was as tender and caring as when he was a child.

"You're tired." Mama sounded wistful. "You've been working so hard. They've put a lot in your hands."

"Have you come a long way?"

"All the way from the bayou."

"Was it hard to find me?" he asked.

"Not at all. I should have come before now. I should have come when I received your letter."

"Did I write?"

She drew back with a laugh. Mama nodded and touched her chest, as if she kept the letter over her heart. "It frightened us, Dad and I."

In the pocket of his shorts, his mobile phone sounded like a bullfrog's groan. Presden removed it, peered at the screen, saw it was Merle and turned the phone off.

"I've missed you," he said, touching Mama's wonderful hair, breathing her fragrance. "You and Dad. And Delphine."

"It was just a scare," Mama said. "A bad dream." She stroked his head. "Nothing like that ever happened. Dad's doing fine, and look at me." She laughed. "Go ahead," she said softly. "Cry all you like."

And he did. He cried for the terror that wouldn't fade, for the loss and the sadness that wouldn't let go. "Delphine," he whimpered.

"She's with us right now," Mama said. "Can you feel her?"

He shook his head.

Mama took his hand and placed it on her middle.

It was rounded and swollen. Presden looked down. "What's happened to you?"

"Well what do you think?" she laughed. "I'm carrying twins. They run in our family, you know."

"But—"

Mama shifted his hand. "That's my baby boy."

How could that be? he thought.

"And this," Mama said, "is my little girl."

Was he touching his sister's brow? His fingertips moved and something flexed, a knee or an elbow.

"I don't have much time," Mama said.

Presden glanced at the wall clock. It was a turtle shell now.

52

Mama stooped, retrieving a canvas shopping bag on the floor by her feet. Before he could stop her, she'd turned and walked through the revolving door.

He hurried after her. "Mama—"

She crossed the street and started along the walkway beside the canal, holding the shopping bag loops with one hand and moving quickly.

"Wait," Presden cried.

As Mama moved, the night air shifted around her. Her hips stirred silver eddies, and her elbows left streaks of foam. His legs were racing, but he couldn't catch up. "Please," Presden begged.

Mama halted without turning. As he hurried forward, the patterns subsided.

When he reached her, she bowed her head, looking down at her feet. "Not tonight," she said.

"Don't leave me."

"I'm staying at the Samen Hotel. Come visit me there."

"The Samen?"

"For lunch." She faced him, nodding. "They have an elegant dining room. What a country. I love these people. And they all speak English."

"Mama—"

"You can't follow me." Her smile was bittersweet. "The Samen Hotel. You be there. Promise."

"I promise."

With that, she turned and continued along the walkway.

Presden watched her go.

As she passed them, the streetlights dimmed. The posts bent, the lanterns drooped and Spanish moss hung down, swaying in the wind. The far side of the canal was muddy and lush with reeds.

Mama's figure was rippling strangely. She held the bag with one hand while the other skimmed the rail. The buildings across the way were dissolving, turning to fog. In the distance, Presden could hear the piping of terns.

Her legs were rubbering now. Her head bobbed, her arms wriggled like snakes. The shopping bag fell from her hand. Then, as he watched, she sank against the rail.

Presden shouted, racing toward her. It seemed the railing had caught her, but before he could reach her, Mama's body seemed to soften and stretch. She passed between the bars like liquid poured from a bottle, and as he halted, the last of her slipped into the water.

A helpless moment—

And then, as she was carried away, he saw her smile on the patterned current. Its soothing curl staggered and spread, while asterisks winked and a scarf of lozenges glittered behind. It was an arm of the swamp, not a Dutch canal. The bubbles rising were bayou bubbles, and the foam on its surface was bayou foam. The silver ribbons were the vanishing trails of water snakes, and the gentle slup was the lapping tide in Teredo Lagoon.

The shopping bag was among the reeds. It was on its side, and the Storybook had spilled out. As Presden approached, the book grew larger, as large as a worn suitcase; and then larger still, the size of a battered trunk. Then the trunk's lid sprang open, and all the creatures he and Delphine knew so well came crawling and leaping and flying out.

When Presden woke, he found himself on the daybed downstairs. He had worked at the kitchen table late into the night, then laid down, expecting to nap. Merle must have roused herself and covered him with a blanket.

It was still dark, and it was quiet upstairs, so he stepped into the kitchen and removed some herring and toast from the fridge. He stood by the table, strewn with reports, chewing and swallowing, reliving his dream. Then he made his way to the basement door, turned the knob and crept down the stair.

The battered trunk was in a damp corner, covered with cobwebs and grime. He undid the latches and raised the lid. The layers of clothing were like bedded sediment loaded with fossils, heavy with memories. He removed them slowly. Near the bottom, beneath a layer of swimwear, was a coral watch cap and a novel about a young sculptor and a sea creature. Then the Storybook appeared, along with a couple of jars and a rusted tin can with a string attached.

He sat on the cold concrete, imagining he was on the bough of the Story Tree, in the cradle of its arm. The book opened to Mr. Stretchy, and when Presden shifted his thumb, there were the Oysters. The court was in session, and the judge was presiding. A green oyster with red hairs was giving testimony. The Oyster Sisters sang all the while. They had beautiful voices.

He and Delphine were there, at the bottom of the page.

3

The Water Board met in a nineteenth century building near the Rijksmuseum, not far from Presden's office. The table was large and round, and a tall grilled window caught the rim of the sun. Presden turned the pages of his report while he spoke.

The diagnostics were unambiguous, he told them. The dike needed major work. He reviewed the results of his tests and spelled out the alternatives. At the Count's request, the dike's demolition was among them.

Presden looked up from his document, ready to answer questions.

An elderly woman raised a jeweled hand and began to speak, addressing a younger man across the table. A gray-headed fellow with vest and spectacles interrupted. They were talking about Holland's past. Something the spectacled man said troubled the woman, and a volley ensued. Another

Board member joined the fray, and the names of neighboring villages were mentioned. The elderly woman looked at Presden, lifting her brows to share her frustration.

He was supposed to be answering questions, but no one was asking any. The Count sat beside him, silent, dipping his beak like a feeding hawk.

The talk shifted to Droomwater, and opinions were voiced about the rebuild. "Extend the foreshore," said the spectacled man. "Anchor bolts would be faster and cheaper," the younger man said. Other views followed, mostly uninformed. Then things took a doomful turn.

A woman with a birdcage veil addressed the group. "I'm not convinced we should repair it," she said.

Silence.

Then the man beside her sighed. "Give it up. Let the water go where it likes." He opened his hands. "We'll have a park—Droomwater Bay. Fishing, boating, wildlife."

The spectacled man was nodding. "You may be right."

And another agreed. "They'll be thrilled to get a premium on market rate."

Presden waited for the Count to speak, but the big man said nothing. It was the elderly woman who disagreed. "I'm not in favor," she said, "of condemning the village."

More silence. Then the younger man took her side, and the consensus dissolved.

When the meeting adjourned, the Count asked Presden to walk with him. As they started across the Museumbrug bridge, Presden spoke.

"I'll be honest," he said.

"Please do."

"I have some pride in my work. I'll fight for the best solution: avoiding shortcuts and false economies, persuading my client to fund defenses against the sea that will do the job long into the future."

"You're a moral man," the Count said.

"You chose me because I live on the dike and I'm close to the problem. But I don't want to lose our home, and I don't want our neighbors to lose theirs. I wouldn't have taken the job if I knew you were going to ask me to justify destroying the village."

"Have I?"

"That's coming, isn't it? I'm ready to resign."

"I don't want that," the Count shook his head.

"Is there a date for a decision? There's no agreement, and half of them seem to be leaning the wrong way."

"You're right to be concerned," the Count said.

A boat passed below them. Presden chose his words.

"Why didn't you speak?"

The Count stopped and regarded him. They were across the bridge now. "The Board has an advisory role. The authority to determine the course of action belongs to me." Beneath his silver brows, the Count's eyes glittered.

"I'm going to pass that to you," he said.

"What?"

"I want you to make the decision. And it needs to be timely enough that we don't put anyone's life at risk."

"That's easy," Presden laughed. "I'm saving the village."

"Your bias doesn't surprise me."

The Count's tone was stern.

"You'll weigh the construction costs," he said, "the long-term integrity of the dike, the impact on our coastline and the other villages."

Presden listened, wondering at the Count's purpose.

"And there are deeper concerns," the big man said. "Important things are at stake here—things that the particularities of currents and seawalls don't address. There are times when the instinct for self-defense is destructive."

Presden recognized the philosophical tone and the lofty abstraction. It was the same nonsense the Count had been spouting when they inspected the breach.

"Shall we commit to defending ourselves forever, or is it time to yield? This is more than an engineering project."

"The things you're talking about aren't my affair," Presden replied.

"They are now," the Count said.

"I'm not going to keep anything secret from my neighbors."

"They should know," the Count nodded. "I want everything out in the open." He looked down at the water in the canal. "That dike is a product of the childhood of man. The monks who designed it had no understanding. For them, the sea was a threat. And the cottages they built— Though they're cherished by some, saving them may not be right or best."

He raised his head.

"In a way—" The big man sighed, wistful, resigned. "We're all living on dikes designed by children."

The Count had a lunch date, so he excused himself.

On impulse, Presden rode the tram across town to the Samen Hotel.

He stood gripping the rail, thinking of Merle while the tram took the bumps. What was he going to tell her? If he shared the Count's words, he could imagine how she'd react. "There are times when the instinct for self-defense is destructive."

The man had some nerve. Caring about his wife's well-being wasn't self-defense. For her, the world was a safe place. He didn't want that to change. It was his duty to protect their home and their life together.

The hotel was on the harbor, a city landmark full of nouveau antiques, painted lanterns and enameled murals. He rode the lift up to the dining room on the top floor. It was a chamber of fantasies, hung with leaded mirrors and jellyfish blown from glass.

The maître d' seated him, unfolded a napkin and set the menu before him. When the man stepped away, despite himself, Presden checked the tables around him.

Then he laughed. What am I doing here? he thought. But he knew: he was there because the dream was so sweet that he wished it were true.

As he ate, Presden thought about the villagers. Telling them would be hard. They didn't know the dike was in danger, much less that their homes might be condemned. It should have given him comfort, knowing the decision was his. But he was nervous about what the Count's request for impartiality meant. If he put forward a plan to repair the dike, and the Count questioned his motivation— What then?

On the way out, to amuse himself, he checked at the front desk to see if there was a woman of his mother's description staying at the hotel.

Merle returned home at 3 p.m. following her appointment with the obstetrician. The doctor confirmed what her body already knew.

She stood on the crest of the dike now, face to the wind, hair stranded across her eyes, watching the breakers and hearing them crash-and-then-hush, crash-and-then-hush.

He can hear the sea, she thought. It was too soon to know its gender, the doctor said. But Merle's intuition was strong. He can hear the shearwaters crying, she thought, and the pebbles and shells clacking in the surf. The idea made her happy, happier than she ever imagined she'd be.

Her heart would be brimming when she shared the news. "We're expecting." That wasn't the right word. They hadn't been expecting. Presden definitely not. He needed time to accept this. And so did she. A new life— An impossible thing.

She turned to look at their house. Pale blue, part of the sky. The paint needed another coat, but even without, the steeply pitched roof and bell-shaped facade was like a home in a fairy tale. His home, she thought. Everything she looked at now, the baby would soon be seeing with his innocent, unblinking eyes.

The cries of the shearwaters reached her again. They were plowing the trenches between the waves, feeding and calling excitedly. An infant needed calm, she thought. Merle slowed her breathing, matching it to the rhythm of the incoming surf. Her purpose in life now was to protect him. Seven more months.

An old man stood on the dike's seaward side, casting his line beyond the surf. Merle thought: What will I hope for when I'm old? Something more than a fish. Maybe a grandchild.

"You're going to be a father." No. Too weighty, too sober. "Presden, it's real, I'm pregnant." That was too much about her. Be coy, be light. Let him share the moment and feel the love you're feeling. "You'll never guess what the doctor said."

Presden spent the afternoon immersed in analytics, reviewing contours and thermal isoliths from the north, replotting the course of the current if the Droomwater dike were rebuilt in this way or that, or if it weren't there. The calculations gave him a feeling of order and a sense of command. But beneath the surface, he was churning. It would be easier to lie to Merle. But he'd tell her the truth. And he'd reassure her. The Count, for some reason, was giving him the power to determine their fate.

He left as the building emptied, and he drove home wishing for a warm shower and a quiet dinner.

The shower was warm, but the dinner wasn't quiet.

"We've made some discoveries about the breach," he began. "The erosion is deep. Deeper than I expected."

Merle continued eating. She seemed distracted. That didn't surprise him. All she knew was that there had been a collapse and workmen were trying to fill it.

"We have infrareds and thermographics now."

She nodded.

"The dike is in bad shape," he said. "Bad enough to need major repairs its entire length."

She looked bothered.

"I should have told you," he said. "I didn't want to frighten you. I had fixes in mind, and I hoped that—"

Merle lifted her head and set her fork down.

She's alarmed, he thought. Wondering where his words were heading. The dike had been protecting the village for centuries, and she assumed it would protect it for centuries more.

"It's not beyond repair," he explained, "but the problems are so severe, the Water Board is weighing other alternatives."

A gust crossed the room and the candle between them flickered.

"I was at the Water Board meeting today." Presden drew

a breath, fearful, expecting a strong reaction. "They don't give a damn about us," he said. Merle had to know. "They were talking about letting the sea take Droomwater back."

Her lips were trembling.

"Fortunately—"

Merle burst into tears and stood. Presden rose with her, but before he could finish, she whirled and headed for the stairwell.

He followed. "I don't know why, but the Count—" They climbed through the dimness, ascending the spiral. "He wants me to make the de—" Did she hear him? Was she listening?

They reached the loft, and Merle stepped forward. A lantern stood on the nightstand, its light flickering on the coverlet and the petals of a morning glory painted on the curving wall above the pillows. Their home, like most of the others, had been built by a fisherman who'd used a design he knew. The ceiling was like an inverted hull, with ribs and a keel.

"Merle—"

She had crossed to the dormer window and swung the casement back. Her head was bobbing with sobs, her shoulders shaking. He came up behind her.

"Don't you want to know?" she whimpered.

He put his hands on her arms, confused. The dike was a black sill, and beyond it, the sea reflected the stars.

"Aren't you curious?" she asked.

In a flash, he remembered. "My god," he murmured.

Merle turned to face him. "Presden, we're going to be parents."

He met her gaze, nodding. He should have been braced for this.

He lowered his palm, setting it on her middle. Merle shivered.

Flesh and blood, he thought. A separate creature with its own heart and mind. Like the twins in his dream of Mama. Defenseless and alive.

"It's a boy," Merle said. "I'm certain."

"I'm sorry, jabbering about the dike. It's my fault."

"There's no fault." She spoke softly.

"I'm going to be a father."

"You are," Merle said.

Presden left the dike path and descended the steps to the dock, eyeing the scroll of surf unwinding on the beach below. Jan was unloading fish from his boat. He raised his head, saw Presden approaching and waved.

The young man went fishing after work. Presden arrived home too late to see the boat leave. But the night before, he'd spotted its lights beyond the surf line, headed back in.

Jan dipped his hand into a bucket, removed a struggling fish and lay it on the planking. His other hand held a knife with a tarnished blade and a silver edge.

"*Bedankt*," Jan spoke to the fish, and he cut its spine to end its suffering. The eyes were gold disks with onyx pupils.

Jan opened its belly like an envelope and swiped the orange slurry of eggs across the wood and into the sea.

Presden removed a flyer from his coat, folded it and put it in Jan's backpack.

"I saw the announcement at the church," Jan said. "How bad is it?"

"We'll discuss that Thursday," Presden replied.

"Something we should be worried about?"

"I'll share what I know at the meeting," Presden said. He'd been going from house to house with his flyers, making the rounds like a postal carrier. It was a relief to visit the neighbors. All Merle wanted to talk about was the baby.

His eye fell on the nets draped over the beams. They were sequined, glittering with scales. The piers on either side were riddled with wormholes.

He stooped, grabbed a red rubber glove beside Jan's bucket and stepped toward the pier. When he pulled on the glove, it looked like a giant crayfish pincer. Presden kicked the pier, using the glove to break away some of the rotting wood. He saw the gleam and the slime and used his ungloved hand to pull a teredo out.

"Look at this," he laughed, dangling the worm in the air.

Jan looked up. "Nasty things."

Afterward they sat in Jan's front room, sipping jonkies. The young couple was renting and the house was sparsely furnished. But in the photos tacked to the walls, they looked blissfully happy. Jan spent his free hours on a bountiful sea, and when the boat was moored, they ate what he'd caught and made love with the surf's lull in their ears.

"By the way," Jan said, raising his glass. "Congratulations."

"Fonelle and I were in the garden," Merle said. "It just popped out."

They were walking side by side on the Droomwater road, headed for the Widow's cottage. Presden held a large cardboard tube.

"You're not angry?" she asked.

"Of course not. I was surprised, that's all."

"It's early," she conceded.

It had been Merle's idea to hold the meeting at the Widow's. The old woman had lived there longer than anyone, and she could be counted on for strong opinions. No one would be more hostile to the idea of giving the village back to the sea. She'd been nosy about the meeting's purpose, but Presden divulged nothing. That afternoon he left a message for the Count, explaining that by the end of the day, the villagers would be aware of the crisis.

The green paint on the Widow's cottage was peeling. Above the front door was a brass casting of a mermaid. A screw had come loose, and she was headed for the deep. Presden knocked.

A moment later the Widow opened the door. Her face

was stiff and humorless, and she was wearing a shirt and trousers. She motioned them in. Without her staff, the old woman tottered, but when Presden offered his arm she ignored it, reaching instead for Merle.

The hall was narrow and the ceiling was low, lower than he remembered. Two dozen people were in the front room, seated and standing. He and Merle stepped through the gathering to a space left vacant for them.

Presden greeted his neighbors, introduced Merle, who they all knew, thanked each for coming, and welcomed Fonelle and Jan to the village.

"As you're aware, the Water Board hired me to look at the breach. And I've been doing some other work to test the dike's integrity. You may have noticed the probes we set. Or the plane last week."

"The Count was here," a man spoke up.

Presden nodded. "He wanted to see for himself."

The room was quiet. *See what?* they were wondering.

"Our dike is in trouble," he said, scanning the faces. Best to be blunt. He needed their trust. "The problems are serious, far worse than I expected. A number of alternatives are being considered, but time is short. Decisions have to be made. Quickly."

"What kind of decisions?" the Widow said.

"That's why I'm here." He looked at Merle.

She knelt on the floor by his feet while he removed the drawings from the cardboard tube. "Let's start with what we know." Merle unrolled a large diagram showing the dike in section. Presden pointed at it as he described the erosion he'd found.

His neighbors looked grave. A few were stunned, disbelieving.

"There are half a dozen ways to repair the dike," Presden said. "We could strengthen it at the point of collapse. We could dredge from the sea floor to fill it, or pack it with inland gravel. But sand and gravel aren't very stable. That could lead to problems later."

"You could build out the foreland in front of the breach," a man volunteered.

"Yes. We could extend the sea side to damp the waves. But that won't address weaknesses elsewhere along the dike. We could shoot anchor bolts from sea side to land side and clamp the dike together. But it would still be peat. Or we could build a new dike from scratch, farther out to sea."

Groans rose from the room. The Widow clenched her jaw.

"I know," Presden said. "Merle and I see the waves from our bedroom. We don't want a view of a pasture with cows. But that solution would be long-lasting. And building a new dike would be less expensive than repairing the old one."

He looked around the room.

"I'm not advocating that approach," he said, "or any of the others I've mentioned. I have a bias. I haven't said anything to the Water Board. I wanted to speak with you first. If I have your support, it will help.

"The surest way to preserve our dike—to make it strong

enough to withstand the sea for centuries into the future—is the most costly. A 'Deep Wall.' We dig a trench down the dike's midline, its entire length. And we fill the trench with concrete and steel. The dike would be gutted during construction, we might be exposed. But once it was done, that would be our best protection."

Mutterings circled the room. Heads were nodding.

"That's what we want," the Widow said.

Fonelle stood. "How can we help?"

"Who needs convincing?" another asked.

"We'll take nothing less," the Widow proclaimed. "The Count needs to understand that."

Presden could have shared what the Count told him—the unlikely delegation, the promise that the decision was his. At the moment, no one knew, not even Merle. But each time he'd debated the question, his doubts had prevailed. He didn't trust the Count's words. If the Board disagreed, who knew what they'd do. How would the villagers react if he told them he had the power to choose and it turned out not to be true?

Presden straightened.

"There's an alternative we haven't discussed," he said.

The room grew silent.

"Droomwater has a problem," he said. "The Water Board has two. The first is that the erosion of the dike threatens our village. The second is that the whole coastline is exposed. The sea is rising, the current is accelerating. Dikes are showing their age in a number of places, not just here. Other villages may be at risk.

"As you all know," Presden said, "the Water Board owns the dike. They can repair it. They can let it fail. Or they can destroy it."

Puzzlement. Fear. They were uncomprehending.

"The land our houses sit on is thirteen meters below sea level," Presden said. "The dunes to the east are sixty meters above. Without the dike's protection, those dunes would become the new coastline, and the sea would create an embayment. The bay would slow the current, and that would take pressure off dikes up and down the coast, protecting other villages."

Stares. Parting lips, open mouths.

"They would sacrifice us?" a woman said.

"They can't do that."

"How long have you known about this?" the Widow asked.

"I learned about it the day he was here," Presden told them. "I was as surprised and as troubled as you are."

"Which way is the Count leaning?" a man asked.

"How could he—" A woman fell to tears.

"We have to persuade him," another said.

"What's he like? Does he have a family, a hobby?"

"He likes drowning villages," the Widow said.

Few found the comment amusing.

Jan peered at Presden. "What did you say to him?"

Presden raised his hands, expressing his qualms, but trying to reassure them. "He was honest with me. He's a thoughtful man. I'm trying to trust him."

"Thoughtful?" The Widow spoke with derision. Her bony face was pale and taut. Presden wondered if it had ever been watered with laughter.

She extended her arm, fingers twitching, as if they could sense something in the air before her. "Forces we can't see," she said, "are playing with our lives."

Waves curled and leaned, the undertow sucking back as the breakers plunged and mixed with the froth. A lone sandpiper galloped across the beach. Presden and Merle were returning from the Widow's, following the path along the crest of the dike. Sheets and towels flapped on a wash line ten feet to land side.

"You were masterful," Merle said.

He wasn't feeling that way. There was too much duplicity, too many questions left to answer.

Presden gazed at the row of houses, shoulder-to-shoulder. They were like a chain of children holding hands, playing crack-the-whip.

"They're with us," Merle said.

A little girl was in the water below. Her parents were trusting to let her swim on her own, he thought. The sky was darkening. She turned bottom up as they passed.

It all seemed so harmless, he thought. The wavelets peaked and slupped, barely whelping. The sea looked calm, its patterns subtle—shadowy rickracks, cords of foam doubling and dividing, feigning tranquility. But the sea didn't fool him.

"You're having a hard time," Merle said, "aren't you."

However pleasing the patterns, he thought, the water was always hatching. Tragedy lurked in its depths.

Merle took his hand. The contact made him shudder as if he'd been struck by a chill from an unexpected quarter. For a moment the trail was a tightrope and he was on it, stepping heedlessly forward, feeling something unknotting inside him.

"Talk to me, please," she said.

I'm here, he thought. I'm with you.

"I'm feeling lonely," Merle confessed. "Maybe that's why I told Fonelle."

Presden barely heard her. A strange idea surfaced suddenly, like the back of the monster in the bayou night, so dark and distressing it stopped his breath: he had lied to Merle when he said he'd be a good father. Her talk of family had opened the way, and hope had loosened his tongue. To win her heart, he'd misled her.

"I need to believe," she was saying, "that we're in this together."

His steps slowed. He peered at her.

"What's wrong?" she said. "Talk to me."

"I'm not sure." He wanted to be honest, but he wanted, as well, to shield her. His thoughts threatened them both, and the unborn child too.

Merle stopped and faced him. She let go of his hand.

"I need you to be close right now," she said. "I can't do this alone. I have to know that you want this baby."

"I do," he said, but his words lacked weight and thrust. "I'm confused."

"About what? It's our dream come true. Isn't it?"

"I thought it would be."

That hurt her. Merle's eyes misted. She turned away.

It was hardly uncommon, he thought—a first-time father, apprehensive, uncertain. How broken was he? The truth, he rebuked himself. A new human was coming to life inside her. He should have felt gladness, anticipation, connection. Instead, the new life felt like a looming threat, a trial to be weathered. The truth, he demanded. And when he pierced the reasoned polemics, searching deeper, much deeper, he found it.

His fears weren't false. Merle's joy was naive. In his heart, he knew.

Presden drew a breath. "I'm sorry," he said.

Merle spoke through her tears. "I can't stop being pregnant. I won't."

"Please— I'm not suggesting that."

Merle put her hands to her eyes. She teetered, as if about to fall. When he reached for her, she didn't resist. But she kept her eyes hidden, and her lips were moving, speaking silently. Who was she speaking to? Her child, he thought. Or the people who had loved and protected her when she was young. *There's no danger or pain in this baby*, Merle told them. *None at all*. Perhaps she was talking about the man she'd married. *He can't be a good father or a good husband either.*

They stood on the darkening path with the sound of the incoming tide in their ears. Beyond the dike, the wind roughed the sea's hackles and smoothed them flat again.

"I'll never leave you," Presden said.

But a part of him had already left.

The moment Presden waved his hand, a taxi pulled up, screeching to a halt beside the curb. Presden opened the door and slid onto the seat.

"Where to?" The cab driver turned.

Presden recognized the Count. "You," he laughed.

The Count took his hand from the wheel, smoothed his mustache and winked. His other coat sleeve was pinned to his shoulder.

"The Samen Hotel," Presden said, glad to be back.

"You're having lunch with your mother," the Count guessed.

"That's right."

And as quick as thought, they were there.

Presden stood on the quay, looking up. With its porthole windows and fin-shaped lanais, the old building looked like a submarine with its nose to the sky.

He entered the lobby and rode the lift up. When he reached the top floor, he passed beneath the vaulted arcades, headed for the dining room door at the corridor's end. As he approached, the double doors flew back.

The place was busy with the lunch crowd, but the maître d' was expecting him. He escorted Presden through the circle booths and S-shaped banquettes. The diners were elegantly dressed, but they were eating possum and snake, frog legs and snails. And instead of fine linen, the tables were matted with lichen.

Mama was seated at a booth in the center, hands folded before her. She was as youthful and vibrant as ever, hair bronze, smile wide. He slid beside her, so glad to see her, so very glad.

Mama put her hand on his. "My dear boy."

Presden struggled to speak. Then he lost his composure and began to cry.

Mama drew closer and gave the tears time. "It's alright." She lowered her brow and spoke softly to him. "You'd like to come home."

Presden nodded. "I would. I'm not happy here."

"It was a blissful time for us," Mama said. "You and your sister—" Her sigh turned into a rueful smile. "She was such a dreamer. I always wondered how she would do in the real world. She was so lost in her imaginings."

Presden wiped his eyes. "She would have done something astounding."

"You're right, I'm sure," Mama nodded. "Shall we go back?"

"Can we?"

Mama rose. "That's why we're here."

When Presden stood, she motioned and turned. He followed.

They wound their way through the diners. Lamps were

drifting around the room like translucent jellies. The floor was puddled with swamp slime, and Spanish moss hung from the chandeliers. They approached the windows overlooking the harbor.

Mama opened a glass door and led him out onto an unrailed lanai.

Far below, the water shimmered, crossed by hypnotic patterns. Silver chevrons skittered like frenzied birds, veering in one direction then another. Fields of diamonds were crushed to nothing and magically restored, every gem sharp-edged and gleaming.

"Remember?" Mama said.

I do, he thought.

She clasped his hand and squeezed it. "Don't be afraid."

"I'm not supposed to go swimming."

"We can break the rules this time," Mama said.

It was a Delphine moment. It asked for blind trust, and the courage she always enforced on them both. Presden closed his eyes.

"Are you ready?"

He nodded.

"Now," Mama said.

And he jumped.

A long moment of silence and suspension. Then a cymbal crashed, a roar sounded in Presden's ears and the water closed over him. Not cold or bracing. It was thick and warm. He held his breath, heart hammering. And then, imagining the element was kindly, he breathed the sea in and opened his eyes.

He could see himself now, unchanged, still flesh, still a man. But his thoughts—his heart and his mind—were transfused with the warmth and a feeling of latitude. He had been a captive, seized and shut in; he was returning now to a freedom that had once been his. The patterns were all around him—ranks of wriggles, lozenges swelling and shrinking, blurring and lapping, hypnotic and luminescent. The magic rickracks stenciled his skin and wove through his body, chafing and smoothing, opening and closing—a thousand fish mouths silently speaking, a million scales spangling and iridescent, reflected, absorbed and shed back into the prismatic deep.

He was settling. His bare feet touched down, feeling the creep of the bayou mud. The shifting patterns clarified, like a tablecloth pulled straight or a shirt Mama ironed. A hill stood in the water before him. A dark hill. As Presden watched, its crest seemed to bristle. The hill was shifting, arching its back, unflexing its arms, unfolding a thick tail.

The Gator, Presden thought, and his heart froze.

The same black beast that had taken Delphine. How long had it bedded here, waiting for him? Its snout turned, and Presden saw the periscope eye.

His grown-up mind wanted to believe an innocent story—that the Gator had no evil intent. But the child knew better. The attack was more than a reflex leap, a scaly arm, senseless claws and giant teeth. The monster had come for them both. It had taken Delphine that night, and it had been hunting for him—the other half of his prize—ever since.

The Gator's black body turned like a wheel before him, its

ridged back flaring, tail sweeping from side to side. Then, as Presden watched, the beast's body was cut by sine waves and carved by swirls. The patterned water divided its flesh, and the Gator jiggered and puzzled apart. A veil of riffles floated past, the monster lost in its glittering folds.

Nothing remained on the bayou floor but a lumpy sack cloaked with mud. A small sack, not much larger than a woman's purse.

"Presden."

A child's voice called.

The sack's lumps moved. There was something inside it.

"Presden. Get me out."

He ventured forward, fearful but hopeful too. Small legs and hands seemed to be pushing, like a fetus in its mother's belly. As he approached, the child's voice deepened and the sack expanded. It was the size of a duffel now.

A fantasy, he thought. Or a trap. Or a gift the bayou was finally returning.

The sack was as large as an oven now, and still growing. A rope was fastened around its mouth.

"Hurry," a woman spoke harshly, impatient.

Presden grabbed the rope, unknotted it and opened the sack, stepping back.

A cloud of silt lifted, and a silhouette rose inside it.

This isn't real, he thought. It was too much to hope for, too much to believe. But he didn't move. He remained fixed in the mud as if bolted there, staring as the silt sifted away. A woman faced him, the sack around her knees.

She wore a beaded gown, lustrous purple, and the beads were thousands of crawling periwinkles. Rings of light moved up her body and descended again. Her arms were slicked with a transparent gel. She held her hand out to him. A pale face with glossy lips— Her black hair was gathered at the rear, caught in a net. He didn't know her. Then she spoke his name, and he did.

"Presden."

The woman gave him an inquiring look and her gravity dissolved. She stepped out of the sack. She was about his age. Exactly his age.

"I know you," he said.

"Yes," she laughed, "I think you do."

Her voice had a different timbre. More buoyant, more husky. She frightened him, but he couldn't look away. She had Delphine's commanding manner, Delphine's confidence— And there was no mistaking: those were Delphine's eyes.

"You'd forgotten me," she said.

"Never."

"You don't have to worry."

"I'm not worried."

Delphine narrowed on him. "Once in a while, you could admit that I'm right."

Presden laughed, and she did too.

"It's really you," he said.

Delphine's netted locks sparkled with bubbles and flowed to the side. She eyed his brow with her coal-fire eyes. "You're taller than I am," she said. "So big. Big lips," she touched them, "big jaw, big face. A man you'd find on a ship."

She turned and scanned the water around them. "Our waking dream. The magic lagoon." She put her hand on his chest. Her nails were pearly. "I wish I had never left."

Presden tried to speak, but emotion choked him.

"I've missed you," she said, "so much."

"I loved you," he sobbed. "More than anyone on earth."

"Remember all the creatures we found?"

"I still have the Storybook."

Delphine's head shifted. Her hand was still on him, but her attention was drawn to something at her feet. A crayfish was scuttling through the silt. She turned, watching a school of baby crappie dart past. Presden could feel her delight. *They're still here*, she was thinking.

It had always been like that. He knew her mind without a word passing between them. Presden touched her shoulder and pointed. Shrimp were floating through the spinning columns of silt.

She faced him, memories of the lost bounty welling in her eyes.

Our magical world, he thought.

A shrilling sound pierced the currents. "Listen," Presden said.

Delphine turned her ear. "The Oyster Sisters," she whispered.

The current behind her was layered with bands, undulating and sandwiched by foam. He took a step forward. "Can you see?"

"There's a cave in those rocks," she said. "It's coming from there."

Through the wavering contours, Presden saw a pale wall and a shadowy arch.

Delphine clasped his hand and smiled her wicked smile, the signal for reckless adventure. She pushed off from the bottom, aiming her crown, and Presden went with her. The twins, at home in the water, swimming together—

The pale wall grew closer. The cave's entrance swelled like a dark cloud. A murky grotto. The Oyster Sisters were suddenly louder.

A gar flexed into view, leading the way. Delphine twitched her nose at Presden, and they arrowed through the cave's ragged opening together. Then the gar plunged, and they aimed their crowns down. Darker, deeper— The Sisters were louder still.

Through the dimness, the beds appeared.

Oysters crowded the walls of the cave, and as the twins approached, their wrinkled shells opened. A multitude of eyes, Presden saw, and they were all dots with oversize lashes, as if they'd been drawn by children. The shells' nacred insides flashed and the cave grew brighter. Then the singing ceased.

"Who goes there?" one of the Sisters said.

They sat on a ledge, shells parted, their delicate frills exposed. They had dark wavy hair and silvery lips, with question marks for earrings.

"We know you," Delphine answered, scanning the walls.

"Remember the twins?" Presden said.

"The twins?" The Sisters' valves opened wide.

"The pirogue," one said. "That horrid night," another sighed. "Who can forget." Then they sang as one, "It was child's play, till the Gator took her away."

"You knew them?" a Sister asked.

"I'm the girl," Delphine said. "I've come back."

Silence. On every wall, the lashes of the Oysters blinked.

"And you?" the Sister turned to Presden.

"I'm her brother."

Presden let go of Delphine's hand. They stood now, a few feet apart, on the cave's gravel. "I grew up," he said.

A Sister eyed Delphine sadly. "Your joys cut short. Your future lost."

Delphine bowed her head.

"And you," another plied Presden. "How was it for you?"

Her tone was jarring. Presden could hear the ire in her voice.

"Well?" the Sisters demanded as one. "How was it for you?"

Presden stared at them, baffled by the challenge. He looked at his sister. There was alarm in her eyes. She shook her head.

"Come on now," the Sisters reproved him.

"How do you think," he said. "It was terrible."

"Suffering, heartbreak? Tell us."

Their question was loaded with irony and contempt.

"My life was empty without her."

"Empty? Really?"

84

Delphine's stinging eyes fixed on the Sisters. "What is this?"

They peered down from their shelf and thrummed in the silence. Then their voices swelled, filling the cave. "His crime," they sang, "cries for justice. We need Big Oyster."

On every side, the shellfish turned toward the cavern's center. There, on an apron of slate, a giant gray bivalve rocked. From between its rumpled lips, large bubbles rose with a sound like burping or snoring.

A cloud of veligers descended on Presden and his sister. Tinkling, they herded the two forward. "The wise, the esteemed," the Sisters sang.

As Presden watched, the bubbles lopped and the rumpled lips parted. The giant lid rose.

"Alright—" Big Oyster bulged, loose eyes rolling in the over-large bowl, looking around. "What's on the docket?"

"The twins," a Sister sang out. "Remember the twins?"

"Delphine has come back," another said. "Things must be set right. The crime must be punished."

Oysters filled the cave with jeers and whistles. "Crime," they yammered, "crime, crime—"

"Quiet," Big Oyster upbraided the colony. "What's your name, son?"

"Presden." He glanced at Delphine. She was eyeing Big Oyster, mystified.

"There's a charge?" The judge turned to the Sisters.

"Deceit," they clamored. "Betrayal, desertion."

"And evidence?" Big Oyster pressed them.

"Lots," the Sisters replied. "Everyone knows, and there's an eyewitness."

Big Oyster regarded Presden, suspicion pooling in his baggy eyes. "Summon the Magisters."

Presden was trembling. He felt weak and small. And, in fact, he was smaller by inches. He was shrinking, and so was Delphine. She stood wide-eyed beside him, silent and still.

Four hoary bivalves were clacking forward. The Magisters settled around the judge, a pair on either side.

"Proceed," Big Oyster glugged.

"Ask him," a Sister suggested, "where he went three days after."

Magister Titus obliged. "Where did you go?"

Presden tried to calm himself. "To Aunt Lenora's."

"Hundreds of miles away," the Sisters sang.

"She lived in the next county," Presden objected. "They were searching the swamp. My aunt—"

"He'd already forgotten Delphine," a Sister railed.

"Give him a chance to tell his story," Big Oyster said.

"I couldn't sleep," Presden said. "I cried and cried. I couldn't stop." He saw the distress in Delphine's face.

Magister Curlis sighed. Magister Right's lip quivered.

"You wanted to help with the search," Big Oyster guessed.

"I did, but they wouldn't let me."

"Lies," a Sister sang out.

"Quiet," Big Oyster grumped. "Then what?"

"They took me home. I went back to school."

"There was sadness and grieving among the children," Curlis guessed.

"Is that right?" Big Oyster said.

Presden swallowed.

"Is that right?" Big Oyster repeated.

"Everyone wanted to know where she was."

"Well what did you say?" Big Oyster asked.

Presden looked at his sister. "I told them you were sick."

"Sick?" Big Oyster said. "What in the world were you thinking?"

Delphine covered her eyes with her hand. It was a teenage hand. She was a woman no more, and Presden was no longer a man.

"Oh it's worse than that," the Sisters sang. "Ask the witness. He was there."

They turned toward the opposite wall of the cove. An oyster glued there had parted his valves and seemed ready to speak. He was small and green with red hairs.

"You know the accused?" Big Oyster asked.

"I do," the witness replied. "After his sister pried me loose, he put me in a jar. I lived on their dock for weeks. I saw the commotion, the police and the boats, when Delphine disappeared."

"The accused wasn't present?" Big Oyster said.

"No. And when he returned, he treated us harshly."

"'Us?'"

"The creatures in jars. He threw us all back."

"Is that correct?" the judge asked Presden.

He nodded. "I never went into the bayou again. Dad burnt the pirogue."

He was even younger now, and the court had more power over him—power a grownup would never have granted it. Delphine was pouting and tearful.

"You aren't being fair," she said. "He wanted to forget. The memories were painful." She grasped Presden's hand. "Can't you understand?"

One of the Sisters addressed Delphine directly.

"You don't know about the game, my dear."

"Game?" Big Oyster grumbled. "What game?" His eyes rolled, admonishing the accusers perched on their ledge. "You're trying my patience, girls."

"He betrayed her," one sang out. "Admit it," they shrilled at Presden together, "admit it, admit it—"

He faced Delphine. Eight years old again, the same age they were the night of the Gator. Fearful, he struggled to speak.

"You didn't betray me," Delphine said.

"I pretended you were alive. I talked to you," he explained. "But that made things worse. Then— I thought of a game."

"What game?" Magister Titus demanded.

"Cruel," the Sisters chorused. "Horrid and cruel."

"Let him speak," Big Oyster said.

"Nobody knew," Presden told his sister.

Delphine watched him, waiting.

The cavern was silent. "Well?" Big Oyster prodded.

88

"I pretended you were . . . imaginary."

Delphine frowned.

Presden drew a breath. "That I'd never had a twin, that you never existed."

A moment of shock, as his words settled in. "I never existed?" Delphine said.

She looked small and alone. Which was greater, he wondered—the pain in his heart or the pain in her eyes?

Delphine began to cry.

"Look what he's done," Magister Right said.

"Shame," the Sisters sang, "shame, shame."

Now Presden was crying too. "Please, don't—" He opened his arms to her. She was limp, but he held her tightly, both of them shaking with sobs. "Forgive me," he begged. "Please forgive me."

"He put her out of his mind," Curlis said.

"Out of my mind," Presden whimpered, "but never out of my heart. I've always loved you. I never stopped."

"Guilty, guilty," Curlis and Flabus concurred.

"Delphine should have been spared," Magister Right said.

"The boy would have been a better victim," Flabus agreed.

Presden barely heard. There was no defense. The charge was true, and there were so many others. He should have kept the pirogue afloat. He should have drawn the Gator's attention away from Delphine. He should have been braver, he should have fought back— What happened to Mama was all his fault, and what happened to Dad was too.

"He must answer for this," Magister Right said.

Presden felt Delphine's lips on his cheek. She drew back, letting water between them, peering into his eyes, seeing his guilt, feeling his pain.

"He blamed himself," she said. "That's why he tried to forget me."

"That's no excuse," Flabus said.

Magister Titus rattled his shell. "Who allowed this reunion?"

"Presden doesn't deserve her," Right said.

Delphine faced Big Oyster. "I don't care what he did. I don't want to lose him."

The Magisters looked to their chief.

"That's the real question, isn't it." Big Oyster nodded his lid. The Sisters began to shrill, but he cut them short with a "hush." Then he pursed his lips, filtering his words. "Does Presden Deserve Delphine?"

"He does," Delphine implored him.

"I'm not persuaded," Big Oyster said. "But your opinion matters. I'll grant him a continuance. He'll be in your custody, and we'll see how things go."

A crashing sound, and a wayward current flooded the court.

The shells of the oysters closed as one, and the surge washed Delphine and Presden out of the cavern.

4

The tomatoes were in, and green tendrils threaded the trellis. Parsley sprouted on either side, chives in front and hydrangeas behind. Merle scooped potting soil from a bucket. The Widow knelt beside her, packing the dark earth around new plantings. The old woman was wearing high boots, and her staff lay by the steps.

"I'm fixing up our spare bedroom," Merle mentioned. "We have a guest coming."

"Staying long?" the Widow said.

"I hope so," Merle replied. She laughed and sat back. "I'm pregnant."

The Widow patted Merle's knee. "Fonelle told me."

"Does it show?"

The Widow shook her head. "Not yet."

"It's a boy," Merle said. "He's talking to me."

"Droomwater is a perfect place for a child."

"I think so too." Merle had met the old woman's daughter.

"Let's hope nothing changes that."

"Presden's working very long hours," Merle said.

"He may not have a say in the matter. He's on the Water Board's payroll."

"The Count respects him."

"I'm sure you're right," the Widow said. "I'm sure he's doing everything he can. You know how I am. I get angry just thinking about it."

"I had no idea," Merle said, "how bad things were. He waited till the last minute to tell me. Presden always does that. It makes me crazy."

"He wants you to feel safe," the Widow said.

"That's it, isn't it."

The Widow nodded. "You're a fortunate couple."

"We are," Merle said. "But our old life is fading." She peered at the ground. "So much has changed, and it's happened so quickly. I imagined I'd be more prepared."

"It was like that for me," the Widow said.

"Was it? Presden's struggling. I don't want to worry myself or my baby, but—"

"But what?"

"It's not that there's any friction between us. It's just this feeling I have. I'm not sure he's ready."

The Widow lifted her shoulders. She seemed about to speak.

"You went through that too," Merle guessed.

"I didn't. He was readier than I." The old woman grabbed

the trowel and started a new hole. "I don't want to meddle."

Merle could see she was guarding her words.

"Tell me," Merle said.

"Maybe I shouldn't mention this. It's probably nothing." The Widow raised her head. "The son of a good friend is a desk clerk at the Samen Hotel. Your husband was there last week, asking about a woman."

"Presden?"

"There's a simple explanation, I'm sure. Some misunderstanding."

Presden returned from work to find Merle upstairs in the spare bedroom cleaning brushes. Her hair was bound up and she was wearing one of his old shirts with the elbows blown out. Two of the walls were baby blue. Cans of paint were stacked in the corner with tarps and solvents, and to one side were the planks and bars of a crib requiring assembly.

He greeted her and stepped closer, kissing her temple.

"You know how much I think about you?" Merle said.

"Too much," he replied.

She poked his middle with the butt of her brush.

"I'm changing these clothes," he said.

He was in the bedroom undressing when Merle entered. She approached the window, looked out at the sea, then turned to the bureau. He'd left the Storybook on top.

She touched the cover. "Remembering."

He nodded.

She waited for more but he volunteered nothing.

"The Widow was here this morning," Merle said, "helping me with the garden. She said something—"

Presden saw the suspicion in her eyes. "What? What is it?"

"The son of a friend of hers is a desk clerk at the Samen Hotel. He said you were looking for a woman who was staying there."

"I was," Presden laughed. "It's crazy, but— I imagined my mother had taken a room. I had lunch at the hotel after the Water Board meeting." He pulled on a casual shirt.

Merle raised her brows. "Was she there?" Then reaching to straighten his collar, "Are you alright?"

He saw the concern in her eyes.

"I've been having strange dreams," he said. "About Mama and Delphine. In the first, Mama came to Amsterdam to see me. In the second, I was with my sister."

"Tell me," Merle said.

"They're the kind of dreams you wake up from wondering if they really happened. In the last, Delphine had grown up. I was on trial."

"For what?"

"Betraying her," Presden said. "Forgetting her."

Merle gazed at the Storybook. "You've never done that." She set her hand on her middle. "Does this have something to do with me?"

"I expect so. Mama was pregnant."

"They're both still with you." Merle spoke softly, as if to herself.

"There's an eight-year-old boy," Presden said, "who's still afraid of that Gator. He can't forget what happened that night. He remembers his twin, how much she meant to him. And he misses her."

"I've always wanted to be the one to fill that empty space," Merle said.

He could hear the sorrow mingled with her care.

"Was there joy, seeing her again?" Merle asked.

"There was," he said. "More than I can express." He remembered standing with her before Big Oyster, how he felt the moment she put her lips to his cheek. The game he'd played to save himself didn't matter to her.

Merle honored his feelings with silence. Then she spoke, slowly, choosing her words. "Maybe the dreams are a sign of renewal."

Presden was silent. What renewal was possible? Delphine was dead. She belonged to the past. He remembered those hysterical nights, the sobbing, the pain, his wish to leave life and what it took to come back.

Merle's hand was still on her middle.

"A parent," he said, "must be a protector."

She nodded. "You're a great protector. You've protected me."

"An infant, a child—"

"I'm not worried," she said.

She'd never wrestled with death, he thought. She had no idea.

"Things can go wrong," he said. "Did your doctor talk about that?"

"He's lucky. I can feel it."

"What about us?"

"I'm lucky too," she said, "and so are you. Because you're with me."

"Terrible things can happen to people. In a heartbeat, life can be taken away."

"We can't worry about that," she said.

"Look around you, Merle. Our neighbors could be washed away. If I make a mistake, lives could be ruined or lost. You're decorating the nursery, planting your garden as if these threats didn't exist."

"Nothing can hurt me," she said, "as long as we're together."

He stared at her stubborn smile. As always, unshakeable. He circled her with his arms. Merle's hope was like a fountain of youth. Someday he'd put his lips to it, and the bliss he'd known as a boy would come again and not be taken away.

She whispered, "I want to be in the water with you."

Fifteen minutes later they were in the chop beyond the breakers. It had been a while, but swimming was a powerful thing for them both. It brought them together.

"How is the class?" he asked.

"Some of the women are huge. One's gained eighty

pounds. I made a decision today," Merle said. "I'm going to do it without drugs."

Ten meters from them, shearwaters were skating in the trenches of foam, their cries borne on the wind.

"He'll be perfect," she said. "A perfect baby born into a perfect life."

With her body beneath the surface, Merle's faith seemed magnified, as if her face was a portrait and all the sky a frame.

"Think of this," she flared her eyes. "He's listening. He knows what we're saying. Not the words. He feels our emotion. Our conversation touches him like a shifting tide."

"I like the idea," Presden said.

"Would you do something for him? Will you tell him you want to be his father?"

When he nodded, she took his hand and placed it on her middle.

"We're happiest when we're young," Presden told his son.

Merle made a patient face.

"I want to be your father," he said. "I'll do everything I can to protect you."

Merle smiled and closed the distance, pressing her body to his. "I don't want a child," she murmured. "I want *your* child."

"There's something you should know."

"Mmm?"

"The Count wants me to render the verdict on the dike," he said.

"That's no surprise. You're the expert."

"Not just the technical analysis. The decision about Droomwater's fate."

"Why would he do that?" Merle wondered.

Presden shook his head.

Silence.

"You see," she laughed, "how lucky we are?"

A weedy lot was opposite the church, on the other side of the Droomwater road. Presden and Merle walked there, greeting others on the way. The community gathered amid a half-dozen rickety tables an hour before the scheduled meeting. It was what would have been called "potluck" in the States—*frikandel*, mustard soup, herring, *stamppot* and *bitterballen*. Concerns and queries were woven through the chat, but Presden kept his reserve and Merle did the same. As twilight settled on the village, the group followed the path to the road and across the church's seashell parking lot.

Presden squeezed Merle's hand, eyes on the dark brick rising before him, the octagonal tower veiled in mist. The Count's car was parked to one side and the driver was reading a book. On the car door was a medieval coat of arms—a lion rearing up, defending itself from waves on either side. The dike's night watchman stood at the church's entrance. Presden nodded to him and escorted Merle through the double doors.

Regular worship had been suspended decades before, but

the church was available for wine tastings and business events, and a visiting minister held services at Christmas. In the cool interior people seated themselves in the pews. Conversation was thin, the atmosphere tense.

Beneath the high point of the vaulting, on a dais, the Count sat on a folding chair. He wore a dark suit and tie. A coil of gray hair fell over his brow. The coil and his missing cape gave him a casual look, but there was noblesse in his silver mustache and acuity in his steely gaze.

Presden led Merle to a vacant spot in the first pew. Then he mounted the dais, nodded to the Count and lowered himself into the empty chair beside the big man.

The Widow Muldar was in the front row. Presden saw Jan and Fonelle right behind her.

The Count rose, head squared over his shoulders, back straight, looking calm and self-assured. He wormed his brows and scanned the assemblage with a smile of recognition, as if he was giving a toast at a family dinner.

"I want to start by saying one thing, and I'll say it as simply as I can. My heart is with you."

The Widow squirmed on the pew, shifting her head as if she was trying to see the web he was weaving.

"Those who work with me know," the Count said, "I love the ancestral villages of our watery land, and I care about the people in them."

The Widow raised herself with a lopsided scowl. "You're an oily snake. You don't care about us." She faced the crowd. "The sea took my husband, but it won't take my home."

The smile below the Count's trimmed mustache was gentle. "Things aren't as you imagine," he said. "Presden has made his recommendation, and I trust his judgment."

With that, he motioned to Presden and seated himself.

Presden stood, scanned his neighbors' faces and shared the good news. "A Deep Wall," he said. "It will be complicated and costly, but we're going to do it."

And with that, the tension dissolved. Relief and glad words spread through the pews. The Widow's lips parted, startled. Then she beamed at Presden, raised her closed umbrella and shook it at him. Merle was smiling, her lower lip folded beneath, holding back tears. Presden had warned her—there was no guarantee the Count would live up to his word. But he had, and no one was happier than she was.

"The Cistercian monks," he told them, "didn't appreciate the strength of the forces they were resisting. Today, we know enough about currents to see their mistakes. And we're going to rectify them."

"Good for Presden," Fonelle cried out.

A man laughed, another shouted his name.

"Please," Presden said, "show your thanks to the Count."

The villagers rose from their seats, and the two men descended the dais to mingle. The Widow reached her bony hand out, grasped the Count's arm and squeezed it. As Merle drew closer, Presden saw her studying the steely-eyed man. The Count remembered her, and he bowed and smiled. Merle stared back, strangely grave, as if the Count knew about the stress this decision had put on their marriage. Presden wondered if she was going to share the message of new life with him. But the next moment, she was at his hip and the Count was moving away.

Returning home, they followed the path along the dike's crest. The sight of the breach was unsettling and Merle was silent. But once the collapse was behind them, she gave voice to the relief she was feeling. Droomwater would survive, and more—the new dike would give it a security it had never had.

Presden listened, watching the water. A wind had come up. He could feel the gusts on his front, and he could see the rippling hatchwork, as if the surface had been roughed to life by the breeze, or by something beneath.

Merle's stock in their safety led to thoughts of their home. She was speaking of her great affection for it, for the garden they'd planted, for the plane tree beside the drive, for the berries that would ripen beside the patio door.

But the sea wasn't listening; and Presden, just barely. The roof of clouds was opening, bars of sun reaching through, playing over the waters. The *lups* were rising, ripples to waves, clashing and crossing.

Merle's thoughts passed from the grounds into the house, up the spiral stair to the nursery. Was he pleased with the color she'd chosen? A mirror on the door would be nice. Their son would dress himself and see himself grow. Had Presden looked at the crib? She was having a hard time putting it together. Could he help?

The foam grew thicker as Presden watched. The water was marbled with it, and the chop continued to lift—a myriad sharp-edged crests, raised and lapped over; a myriad splashes, like heartstruck gasps, froth on straining lips; while the souls beneath yearned and the seabirds cried.

Merle was talking about clothing. Her diet. Strange food cravings. Then she said "Deep Wall," and in a stroke, the sky closed and the sun vanished. In the dimness, it seemed the magic had ended. The cresting waves, the breathless splashes, the garlands of foam— The patterns were lost.

A Deep Wall, he thought. Freedom from fear. Absolute calm. That should have brought him comfort. But it didn't.

In an instant, more than anything, he wanted to see his twin, to be with her again, to talk and touch, to believe—if for only an hour or two—that the bliss he'd known as a child hadn't been lost.

"Presden? Are you listening?"

"Yes, of course."

He hoped Merle was still immersed in her litany, but he could tell from her silence that he'd broken the spell.

"What are you thinking about?" she asked.

"My sister," he said.

The sound of the water reached him. Had he left the dormer window open? Sometime in the night, the wind had shifted. *I should get up*, Presden thought. If he didn't, the sound would wake his wife.

But he didn't move. In a corner of his mind, suspicion spoke. Lingering doubt, the whisper of reason.

The sound of the waves mounted, growing louder and louder.

The flood siren went off.

Presden threw back the sheets and sat up in bed, listening to the wowing siren and the thud and rumble of waves against the house. What had happened? Where was the night watchman? Had he abandoned his post?

He stood and joggled the wall switch. The overhead light came on. The force of the waters shook the house and rattled the windows. Somehow Merle was sleeping through it. The bedroom door was open. Presden looked into the stairwell.

He could see the treads of the spiral stair, and the water—green and frothing—rising over them, drowning the shelves of books on either side.

Merle, he thought. He had to wake her. But his senses were caught by the water in the stairwell. The green hoops were circling, bobbling and lifting an object: a rusted trawling can with a string trailing behind. Was his sister near?

His longing was fierce. He couldn't resist it. *Delphine*, a voice inside cried, *Delphine, Delphine*—

The flood topped the last tread. The ground floor was swamped.

This is my doing, Presden thought. It was too late now to protect his home.

The water touched his feet, thick and warm, bringing

memories of the contact he yearned for. The dormer window was open. He sloshed toward it, seeing a night sprinkled with stars. The dike was crumbling. The sea had risen against it. Giant waves had eaten away large pieces, and the surf was breaking against the houses.

The siren warbled and choked. Silent. Drowned.

The end had come all at once, without his suspecting.

Presden felt himself held and supported. And then suddenly he wasn't. The floor of the loft was waterlogged. It parted like cheesecloth beneath his weight.

Down he went, down into what he feared most—feared and desired. The dark and the depths pulled him under and bore him away.

He was moving quickly, tumbling over and over. Was it the churn or the currents, or his disordered senses? Ranks of chevrons, vees and diamonds swelling and shrinking, flaring and fading, reappearing in fresh alignments. His trunk flexed, his legs twisted, arms flailing— The sea's lines pierced his skin, tatting his thighs, needling and pulling silver threads through his chest.

Delphine, his twin, the one he needed. Was she near? The patterns ahead wove and rewove—glittering lines, fluid and tremulous, pulsing and stretching, leaving iridescent trails. Would he find her again? Or was she nothing but an illusion he'd spun from the sea?

For a moment, he felt like he did that night in the bayou. His memories of her were laced with fear. Had he heard a word or a wheeze? Or had she just vanished? Was it only the Gator he'd seen? Here he was in the dark again, searching, seeing nothing but empty depths, hearing nothing but his own failing breath.

He'd let go of his wife and his future without a thought. The sea, so long held back, had achieved its true level. The dike had collapsed and the houses were flooded, and in every watery window Delphine's face floated, an image that wouldn't fade. Her waving hair, her gleaming eyes, her remembering smile—

Something in the water ahead. A tulip bulb framed with curving lines. A head first, then a body behind, indistinct but approaching.

Closer, closer—

The lines, silver-white, were ropes cast toward him, circling his body, tensing and tightening, drawing him closer. Was it her?

Lines, glittering lines. Bright ribbons like fins or razor pinions, streaming from her shoulders, her hips and her reaching arms.

"My brother," she whispered, "my very own."

Delphine, he sobbed. *Oh Delphine*—

"I missed you, I missed you—"

Don't ever go, he thought.

"I won't," she said. "Not ever."

His twin was fully grown, as she'd been when he loosened the rope and she rose from the sack. Bright patterns fringed every inch of her body—rays of them collared her neck, shawls of them hung from her shoulders, combs of them strung from her open arms, stranding into the darkness.

He embraced her.

"Do you like me like this?" she asked.

I do, I do.

"We look the same age."

We are, he replied.

"Not really."

Her denial echoed inside him.

"Do you know what it's like, being a woman?" she asked.

Presden shook his head.

"Neither do I," Delphine giggled.

Her mirth belonged to a young girl. As it entered his head and settled inside him, it seemed to reshape him. His vision foreshortened. His perspective dwindled.

Delphine's eyes glinted. "Let's be little again."

"Okay," Presden replied.

He wondered: did she mean for good? Delphine was shrinking, and so was he. The future faded quickly. The emotion of youth welled inside him, playful, intense.

She giggled again.

He poked her middle and giggled back.

"Remember," she whispered, "remember . . ."

A child again, she turned and kicked off, launching herself through the patterned sea. Presden swam after.

It happened quickly, without even thinking. The tide of memory infused his mind. Snakes and barnacles, turtles and gars, shrimpies and snails, a paddle and pole and a zooful of jars. He could feel the currents ganging and summing; he could see the whorls of liquid diamonds—turquoise, lime, navy and gold—rotating close, facets melting, crushed and dissolving; while inside his child's chest, mansions of emotion, encrusted and glittering, were built and eroded.

Delphine passed through a cloak of bubbles and it caught around her shoulders. Like a mermaid, Presden thought. His body was so much lighter. And the trouble that had crowded his mind— It had rippled away.

She stopped, treading water, the cloak sliding down. A magic girl, not a grim adult—as joyous as he was to feel her freedom. His impulsive twin, blind to risk, eager to stray. Her mind a fistful of sparklers, her heart was a cherry bomb flying to pieces.

"I'm Mr. Stretchy," Delphine said.

"No. Me."

"Me first," Delphine said.

"Well, okay."

Delphine closed her eyes. "Close them," she said.

Presden lowered his lids. But then he raised them a little. He wanted to see.

"Mr. Stretchy," Delphine called. "Mr. St-r-e-t-ch-y."

A moment later, Presden spotted him.

The translucent worm was wriggling through the currents, headed toward them: a bayou teredo, a living wand of thrills and fantasy.

As the worm approached, it grew and grew, and by the

time it was hovering in the water before them, it was as tall as they were.

Mr. Stretchy's body was slimy and ancient. Its tail fluttered. The big end was its head. As Presden watched, its strange mouth gaped.

"I'm going to drill you with holes," Mr. Stretchy announced. His voice was like Delphine's, but gruffer. "Are you ready, young man?"

Presden sniggled. "I'm ticklish."

"Hold still," Mr. Stretchy said.

Presden felt the giant worm slide against him. On either side of its yawning mouth there were clamshell blades. The teredo's skin was clear and slick. The rickrack currents were bending and circling. Blue rhomboids pulsed above Presden's head. Delphine's Stretchy voice reverberated through the patterned sea. "Hold still," it said again.

"Don't be a monster," he begged.

"It won't hurt one bit," she promised.

The blades in Mr. Stretchy's mouth quivered. The head craned toward him.

"Stop," Presden insisted, feeling the familiar dread. Mr. Stretchy was so slimy—

He raised his arms, but the giant head switched between. He could feel it sliding beneath his chin. Its mouth gripped his chest, then its head was twisting.

"Just a kiss," Delphine laughed.

But it was more than a kiss. Presden felt pain, sharp pain— Like a cold screw turning, Mr. Stretchy's head rotated against him, razors cutting. The warm sea filled the hollow in his chest. The worm stiffened and twisted deeper, burrowing in—

Presden cried out.

The worm turned its head one way and the other. Presden could feel Mr. Stretchy's body crooking inside him, consuming what it was cutting away.

"Stop," he glubbed, "stop, stop—"

But the worm was hungry and heedless. He ate through Presden's body as if it was a tasty pier, leaving a labyrinth of winding tubes behind. Mr. Stretchy's visible part grew shorter and shorter. Finally the fluttering tail disappeared.

"It's nice in here," Delphine said. She sounded surprised.

Presden's mouth gaped.

"Lots of room," she said approvingly. "Plenty of holes."

"Come back out."

"No," she said half to herself. "I think I'll stay. I like it."

"I can feel water inside me—moving. It's creepy."

"You're scared," Delphine said.

"No I'm not."

"You were always afraid of water."

"No I wasn't. It's not me. It's your fault. It's because of you and the Gator."

His words echoed through the wormholes she'd drilled.

"I'm sorry," Delphine said. Her voice was lower, and the mind behind it seemed broader and deeper.

I'm the one who should be sorry, he thought.

And the thought was a man's thought, not a child's. They

were returning, Presden realized. Growing older together.

He looked down. His trunk was expanding, his legs were longer.

"Oh," Delphine said, "I like this. It's even better. There's so much room in here now. We all need room for another inside us."

What was she saying?

"Did you give up when I left?" Delphine asked.

"I don't think so," he said.

"You haven't changed. I know my brother."

"I've missed you so much."

"I'm still here," she reminded him.

Was it Delphine he felt, or the currents?

"We touched the soul of things," she said. "Our home, our water—"

He could never forget, Presden thought. In the pirogue, or on the branch of the Story Tree, or in Teredo Lagoon under the stars, weightless, suspended and drifting.

The pain from Mr. Stretchy's drilling had faded. What he felt now was warmth and fullness, and the buoyancy of water.

"Our home, remember . . ."

It was not like swimming or floating. He was tunneled inside, and the water—all silvery-green, with its rippling chevrons and frothing beads—was passing through him. "Remember," she whispered, "remember . . ."

Was it really Delphine inside him?

He imagined, for a moment, that he was hearing the voice of the sea.

5

The wind was like a nosy neighbor, knocking on the windows.

Presden opened his eyes. Morning light filtered into the room through the dormer curtain. The bed beside him was empty. He could hear Merle downstairs in the kitchen. He was back in the real world, with its hazards and disappointments.

The vault of the loft rose over him, the ribs and planks of the inverted hull the fisherman had built. He remembered that moment in the boat with Merle, their hope for the future, the fantasy ship he would sail across the seas. Then he thought of the overturned pirogue, and the clouds of dark smoke that twisted up when Dad burned it.

Presden drew back the sheets, seeing the conflict clearly.

He had imagined Merle was like his sister. He'd tried to believe that a wife and a family would be enough. And now, in his dreams, he was back with the one he loved most. He was who he wanted to be.

Presden zipped his pants and buttoned his shirt. Merle had told him a hopeful story. He'd repeated it to himself, wishing it might be true. He sat on the bed and pulled on his boots. Still hoping, he thought, still wishing.

Merle, his wife. The woman he'd married. And a child too. It was all so unfair to her. He remembered the game of pretending he'd played as a boy. He was playing another game now. The game was Delphine-is-alive, and it had to end.

He was about to start down the stair when he saw the door of the nursery was ajar. He nudged it open and stepped in. The walls were all painted. Merle had affixed a mirror to the back of the door. The silvered glass started at his feet and stopped at his waist. On the floor at the room's center was a toolbox and the pieces of the crib.

Presden knelt, touching the wooden base and the pile of bars. He stared at the toolbox, then opened it, feeling the holes the teredo had cut in his body. The sea was gone, and there was nothing in its place. The space Delphine had taken inside him was empty, a part of himself that would never return.

He fitted bars into one of the rails, then attached the assembly to the crib's floor. There were things a man had to do to live in the world. All that remained of Delphine were memories. Merle was real. In the kitchen, the tap was running. He heard the clatter of utensils. He set the crib down. It had two walls now. An absurd idea, he thought, that a wooden jail could safeguard a child against the things that threatened it.

Presden stood and descended the spiral stair, remembering how the dream waters rose while Merle lay asleep on the bed. Private dreams, dangerous dreams. He reminded himself of the harmony he and Merle felt when they swam together. They had always been close.

He entered the kitchen. Merle was in her robe, fixing breakfast. Her hair was held by a clasp at the rear.

"Sleep well?" she said, turning toward him.

Presden nodded.

"Delphine again?"

"Yes," was all he could say.

Through the window, the sun was rising. Scallops of light crept across the floor.

"I wish I could join you," Merle said. "I'd like to meet her. Are you hungry?"

"Thanks, but no."

"Did she boost your spirits?" Merle's voice was toneless.

Presden didn't reply. The truth was too cruel. He stepped closer, reaching his arms to embrace her.

Merle put down a pan. "You can share what you're feeling. I might understand."

He lowered his hands. "You're seeing the doctor this afternoon?"

She nodded. Her robe parted, and a slice of her body appeared. "I want to be here, not in a hospital. He's recommended a midwife."

"If that's what you want," he said, "that's the way it will be."

113

He tried again to embrace her, and this time she let him. As he turned his head, something caught his eye by the back door.

"What is that?" he wondered.

There was a puppet on the kitchen floor.

Merle drew away. "I found it washed up on the beach."

It was a sea-tossed thing in a sailor's suit, faded, chipped and armless.

"I'm going to put it in the garden," Merle said. She looked up at him.

"Presden—" Her voice sounded weaker now, reedy and failing. "I'm feeling so much distance between us."

He met her gaze. "Don't worry." Presden touched her chin and kissed her cheek.

Then he took his wool coat from the hook and stepped toward the door.

Outside he ascended the stone steps, cupped and pitted by the boots of fishermen who'd lived there centuries before. On the slope beside him, the first green tomato hung from the trellis. At the top he turned onto the path, following the dike's crest, the sea on his left, homes on his right. A brief rain had fallen before the dawn. Presden stepped around puddles, seeing two children in rubber boots, chanting and jumping to see who could make the biggest splashes. What fun it was to play on the wall between land and sea. The kids laughed and went running for home.

He scanned the water as he rounded the bend. The sun flashed, the clouds parted, and the color shifted from blue-gray to green. Something was bobbing between the waves. He thought at first it was a giant fish or a whale's fluke. But when he pulled the binoculars from his pocket and looked through them, he saw the black mass and the flaking edges of a huge block of peat.

Presden hurried forward, toward the breach. The crew hadn't yet arrived. The gap had turned into a gorge, he saw.

Breathless, he circled it, listening and watching.

And then— He might have been sleeping, dreaming.

Presden looked up and saw a giant wave rising like a mountain from the sea.

His breath froze, his heart kicked as if it would leap from his chest. The wave was a monster, a miscreation of tides. It was headed for the breach like a sign of judgment, as if Droomwater's fate had been decided long ago.

Presden turned his back on the monster and raced down the dike's land side, digging into his pant pocket. By the time he reached the walkway that led to the church, he was shouting into his mobile phone.

He turned and saw the wave strike the dike. A fountain of froth spouted up, the sea curled in the air, and a great comber crashed down. Like black lightning, cracks rayed from the breach in every direction. Hillocks of peat collapsed and large pieces broke off, heaving in the backwash. The sea found the opening and came rushing through.

It hooked to the south, edging the home next to the Widow's. The couple who owned it— The house quivered, windows shattering. A groan and the structure pivoted, torn from its foundations. It leaned over, its pitched roof spreading like the wings of a bird. The back fence bristled, like something alive. The billy goat was tangled in it, thrashing, screaming.

Then the flow forked, changing course. One arm bent around the Widow's home. Her garden slid away, the soil was stripped from beneath her cellar and water rushed below her kitchen window. The other fork was headed toward the church.

In his roiled state, Presden imagined the wave was an expression of things inside him, dark and churning, finally set loose on the world.

The humps of the swells were silver and the hollows were blue. On either side of the boat's prow, the dike stretched, its tiles flashing like scales on a dead fish's flank.

Presden stood with the skipper on the bridge of an old trawler. The throttle was open wide, and the trawler was headed for the breach in the dike. The two men wore yellow flotation vests. Presden had his phone to his ear.

"He's right behind us."

"Good luck," the Count said. "This is your show." And the line went dead.

His show, Presden thought. How had that happened? He'd shored up a failing seawall in Jersey. But that was nothing like this.

On the boat's deck, amidships and aft, sandbags were

piled, and through an open companionway more bags were visible below, stacked against the bulwarks.

Whop-whop. Whop-whop.

Presden looked over his shoulder. The helicopter descended, fighting the wind, struggling to keep its position behind and above the moving boat.

Not far from the helm where he stood, atop the sandbags, was a basket of red webbing. They'd secured cables from the rim of the basket to a steel ring six feet above. Attached to the ring was a steel line that rose into the air toward the chopper's belly.

Presden tuned out the hiss of the helm speaker and the barks of pilot and skipper. Only the roofs of the houses were visible over the dike. The Widow's was intact, but the two homes beside hers were gone. Through the breach, he could see the church tower. A moat surrounded it, and streams were flowing toward the village's north end.

"Dead ahead," the skipper shouted.

Don't veer, Presden thought. And don't lift off too soon.

The black hillocks of the crumbling dike loomed on either side, larger and larger. The boat was making for the low point between. Thirty meters, twenty—

A throaty sound, loud and deep. Presden searched the gap, breathless, trembling.

The skipper barked at him, jockeying the wheel.

The chopper's backwash was fierce. It was directly over them, engine droning. Presden clung to the bridge. Keep on, he thought. Keep on—

Suddenly the throaty sound was a roar, and the drone of the chopper was lost. A section of dike came loose and tumbled toward them. "Keep on," Presden cried.

The skipper saw the bow wave building, and he drove the prow straight at it. The boat heaved up. Hang on, Presden thought as the helm headed skyward—a blast of spray, a hundred pins pricked his face—then the boat was plunging. Waves poured over the foredeck. The prow slammed into the dike, toppling him. The skipper buckled beside him.

"Let's go," Presden yelled.

He rose, scrambling down from the bridge. The boat wasn't moving, but its throttle was wide open. *Whop-whop-whop.* The chopper's backwash tore at his clothes, and its droning made the deck gear rattle. He clambered into the red basket. As the skipper joined him, the boat lurched onto its side.

"Now—" Presden waved his arm.

The chopper rose. The cable went taut. Then the basket rose into the air.

Presden's heart chugged and his vision blurred. Clear, he thought, praying they were. *Whop-whop. Whop-whop.* He looked down, trying to focus.

The water foamed and churned beneath them. Amid the chopper noise, a hollow thud sounded. The boat was heeling over. The basket swung with the two of them in it. Above, the chopper coughed and careened, hoisting the cable. Presden could see the pilot in the cockpit and the aureole of the turning blades. The backwash was fierce. He felt it caving his cheeks, tearing at his hair.

The belly hatch of the chopper was opening. Hold on, he thought.

Then the *whop-whop* dimmed.

The basket rose into the cabin and the hatch closed.

Men in uniform helped him out of the basket. One removed Presden's harness. They were doing the same for the skipper. Presden tried to speak, but words wouldn't come. He grabbed hold of a hash-marked shoulder, swaying, taking unsteady steps across the steel floor.

When he reached the hatch-bay window, he looked down. The chopper was circling over the dike. The ugly new kink, the deep gash of the breach— It seemed to his scrambled senses like nothing so much as the scar on his chest. The pain was still there: the Gator's gift, the pain that started beneath the scar and spread down his middle, into his legs.

His home lay farther along the dike. Merle hoped to give birth to her child there, imagining she'd be safe and protected. Still unaware of the depth of defeat and weakness in the man she'd married.

With a shaking hand, he retrieved his phone and called the Count.

When the big man answered, Presden found his voice. "It's done," he said.

"The boat is lodged in the breach?"

"It is."

"The flooding has stopped?" the Count said.

"Most of it, from what I can see."

The Count sighed. "So the water has settled the question."

The words shook Presden. They seemed to mock his devotion to Merle, and the tone of surrender breathed life into an old indignation. "We can still save the village," he said. "We've lost some homes, and we may lose more. But it's not too late."

"That couple's house—" The Count was doubtful. "They might have been inside. We need to get your neighbors out of there."

"We will," Presden said. "We'll evacuate everyone." He checked the time. "Give me twelve hours. As bad as it looks, it can be repaired. I'll have a plan for you first thing tomorrow."

Silence. Presden imagined the Count shifting to face him. The commanding lips parted, the weighty brow creased.

"Twelve hours," the Count agreed. His voice was brimming with irritation.

"I'm sorry it's come to this," Presden said.

"It shouldn't fall to you and me," the Count replied, "to correct a wrong step that was taken eight centuries ago—a map some Dark Age monk sketched on linen. But failing to protect our people—*our people, Presden*—that's on us."

And with a *click*, the Count disconnected.

The chopper turned, bucking the wind, putting its nose to the south and its head down. Presden called Merle. She was in her car, on her way to the doctor. He explained what had happened. He was heading home, and he'd be there waiting. They'd be safe, he assured her, at least for the night. As they spoke, Presden scanned the village below. It was mostly dry land, but the relentless sea was gnawing, eager to stretch out in the place it once had, the place it still wanted and to which it meant to return.

The chopper set down in the weedy lot beside the Droomwater road. The hatch opened, and one of the uniformed men helped Presden step down. Then he was hurrying from under the rush of air and the cutting blades.

There were neighbors on the road, alarmed, with pressing questions. Presden waved them away and quickened his step.

He was seated at his desk in the living room. His computer was open, and reports lay shuffled to either side. There was a plan on the screen before him, with numbered steps, headings and text. But Presden wasn't typing.

He'd begun with resolve, knowing he had the technical command to solve the problem. Containing the breach raised challenges. Excavating for the new wall raised more. But it wasn't the engineering issues that blurred his focus. It was fear—the unexplainable sense that his expertise didn't matter, that what was happening was deeply personal, that the dike was failing because of him.

His dreams had reduced him from a man to a boy. And the boy's unreasoning fear—never quiet or far—was circling. Fear of the sea's unyielding strength. Fear that his reckless longing would bring his twin back. Fear that the threat to Merle and her unborn child came from him.

He felt as he had when they broke the rules and went

swimming in the bayou. Always the one to stretch the limits, Delphine would kick and swirl away, leaving only the prickle and suck of water, and a vacuum for the one who remained.

He was treading and tilting, panic blooming. There was nothing to grab onto. He was afraid he would sink and vanish.

Like then, he was sensing the calamity before it happened. As if the real moment was already past, and he was only a ghost with a used up life, remembering.

There was a change coming, an inevitable change—the return of the sea, and the land's submersion. The embayment of Droomwater. An unpayable debt, put off for centuries, would at last come due.

Presden could see the future, and it was just like the past. The coastline was ragged and bitten, the village gone, as if it had been devoured by the Gator. And the people, *our people*— Where were they?

The sound of an engine reached him, then it died. A key turned in a lock. Someone opened the front door and stepped down the hall.

He rose slowly and turned, seeing Merle hurrying toward him.

"You're okay?" she said.

She put her arms around him, peering into his eyes. "There's a lake around the church. Is it safe to stay here?"

They'd bought some time by plugging the breach, Presden explained, doing his best to inhabit the man. "The dike can be saved," he assured her. He glanced at his desk. "I owe the

Count a plan by tomorrow morning."

"You've done everything you could," she said. "How could you know?"

The boy inside Presden didn't believe a word she was saying.

Merle grasped his shoulders. When he met her eyes, he saw the same courage he'd seen years before, in the dory after she squeezed the water out of her hair.

"I love you, Merle. I don't want to lose you. Maybe we should move inland."

His words puzzled her.

"I'll find other work," Presden shook his head. "We'll have a family then."

"Then?" The color left her face.

"What I meant was—"

"I'm keeping this baby." She turned her cheek. "I can support myself without your help."

For a moment, Presden wished that he'd sunk to the bayou bottom that night, his heart unmoving, the last air bubbles fled from his mouth and the darkness closed in.

"I've lived my life in the throat of the sea," he muttered. "I made water my enemy because it took my sister away. Losing once—that was enough."

"What happened last night?" Merle said. "What exactly?"

Her eyes were hard.

"What did she say," Merle wanted to know. "What did she do?"

"We were kids again. In the water."

A long exhale exited his lips. And with that breath went all his care, and his compassion too. The secrets he'd guarded were cruel, but what could he do?

"I was happy," he said. "The happiest I've been since the Gator took her. She turned into—" The thought of it made him laugh. "Mr. Stretchy."

Merle's lips were straight, her look disbelieving.

"She drilled me full of holes. And when the sea rushed in—" Presden stopped himself.

His wife was fathoming, finally, the depth of his wound and what it could cost them.

"You have to let go of her." Merle's tone was harsh. "You have a wife who loves you. A little boy inside me. You can't let your dead sister's memory destroy us."

Presden bowed his head.

"It's time to bury Delphine," Merle said.

How doomful those words sounded.

"I'm sorry," he said. And with that, the adult inside him took back control.

"I have an ultrasound on Thursday," she said. "I've been through all of this alone. I want you to be there, to see his heart beating. Promise me."

"I promise."

"The Widow's place— It looks alright from the road," Merle said. "This must be hard for her." She glanced toward the back door.

"Go ahead. I'll be fine."

To ease her doubts, Presden seated himself at his desk and returned to the plan.

The old cottage still stood on the dike, refusing to move. All of its walls were intact, and the roof hadn't shifted. But there was water now in the ground floor rooms.

"Where will you sleep?" Merle said, supporting the Widow with her arm, helping her toward the small kitchen table.

"The attic is dry as a bone," the elder replied. "I've put the sofa cushions and blankets up there." She had a small pot in one hand and a large spoon in the other. "Get the bowls for us, will you?"

As the Widow settled herself, Merle put the bowls on the table and sat across from her, feeling the cold sea in her shoes. The water in the kitchen was four inches deep.

"You're so trim," the Widow said, ladling chowder into the bowls. "Do you ever eat?"

"It goes right through me."

"You're eating for two now."

The Widow set a bowl before Merle and moved the lit candle between them.

Merle could see the entrance to the front room. "You were devoted to each other," she said.

The Widow nodded. "When he returned at night, I always

had food on the stove. I'd pull off his boots, massage his cold feet and rub oil into his chapped hands. He'd sit in that chair, staring at the bottle of beer I'd opened, too tired to drink.

"Sometimes he'd give out on the sofa with his dirty clothes on. I'd leave the stove door open and pull a quilt over him."

"It must have been hard to lose him," Merle said.

"Forty-two years," the Widow sighed. "A poor swimmer. He insisted on sailing at night. It was a cold November. No moon, just fog and stars. My bad knee was itching. I tried to discourage him, but he went anyway."

Merle felt tears coasting down her cheeks.

"Oh dear." The Widow reached out and took her hand. "We're still here, we're still fighting. If Presden can—"

"It's not that." Merle shook her head. What could she say? It seemed so hopeless. Was the sadness she felt anything like the loss that haunted Presden? Was there anything she could do to make it go away?

"I don't think he wants," Merle said, "to be the father of our child."

A moment of silent surprise. Then dismay soured the old woman's face.

"With the breach has come misfortune," she said.

Her words were bitter, as if an old suspicion was being confirmed: the sea was not to be trusted. It had taken her husband and, given the chance, it would take them all.

The Widow looked through the kitchen window. They

could hear the surf, the boom and crash of the angry waves, and the discord of squabbling gulls.

"When we're young and full of romance," the Widow sighed, "what do we know about the husbands we choose?"

Merle felt weak. She was on one side of a cracked door, holding it closed, and the old woman was pushing against it.

"Is he really the man you want to be married to?" the Widow asked.

The words rattled through Merle like a wind through the reeds. Maybe they were going to lose everything—their home, their child and each other.

The Widow's features relaxed. "You're a brave woman," she said. "You could raise your baby without him, if you had to."

Merle closed her eyes. She couldn't imagine that Presden would leave her. And she couldn't imagine leaving him. Being an athlete she was prone to believe that will alone could solve almost anything. One's goals began to recede only when one gave up or slowed down. If she was strong enough, Presden would come around.

The Widow was listening to the wind and the waves. She faced the sea, then she grabbed her staff. "Shall we have a look?"

The two sloshed down the flooded hall and passed beneath the door's lintel. Outside, the Widow led the way up the streaming steps, around the heaped muck, past a large cake of peat that had lodged against her north wall. The breach in the dike was a large ravine now, and they gave it wide berth, skirting the hunks of soaked soil until they reached a level spot where they stood together, watching the dike and the waves crashing against it.

"Eight hundred years," the Widow said. "The seas were lower then, and the nights were colder."

Merle gazed at the trawler lodged in the gap with its hull bashed in, feeling how time was pressing on her. Every second that passed carried her closer to the joy of her son's arrival. But the fear she was losing her husband weighted her heart with despair.

"You can spend the night with me if you like," the Widow said. "There's room upstairs."

"I don't want to do that," Merle said. They had never slept apart in anger or confusion. Not even once.

"If the man's not with you," the Widow said, "you're better off here."

After Merle left the house, Presden found his toughness. The look of betrayal in eyes that had been so trusting seemed one with the guilt he'd borne most of his life. Guilt and the pain the Gator had dealt him. But he knew how to resist. So with the wind rattling the windows and the waves pounding the dike outside the back door, he completed his plan for the Count. A document lay on the desk now, beside his computer.

Presden exited the house, climbed the stone steps and stood facing the sea, waiting for his wife. Minutes later, her silhouette emerged from the dimness. She looked worn. Her shoes and feet were flaked with peat and black to the ankles.

When she reached him, she halted and nodded. "She's alright."

They descended the steps in silence. As he opened the door, she spoke.

"How long will that boat plug the hole?"

"Take off your shoes and I'll wash the muck off."

Red underwing moths circled the porch light. Merle crossed the threshold with one hovering over her shoulder. Presden sat her down and damped a dishcloth. She removed her shoes and handed them to him. Then he knelt and cleaned her feet.

"How long do you have?" she asked.

He glanced at the clock and shook his head. "I need some sleep."

As he rolled up her cuffs, he saw Merle scanning the shelves, eyeing the canned goods and plates as if she'd never seen them before. Then she shuddered and began to cry. "It might be better if I stayed with the Widow."

Presden took her hand. "Please. I don't want to be alone."

She swallowed and wiped her cheek. "I don't either."

They climbed the spiral stair to the loft and undressed. Presden set his alarm for his call with the Count, then they lay down together.

She fell asleep first. Her head was on the pillow two feet away, facing him. Presden admired her through the dimness, the prominent curve of her lips, her creamy brow, her steady breath. Inside her surface poise was a somber courage, a pilgrim determination.

He thought about what she'd said, about burying his sister. Was there any way to forget Delphine, to cast his love and his lot with Merle and a future perched on this crumbling rampart? What would happen when his waking thoughts ceased? At the border of dream, would his twin always be waiting?

Presden put his hand on Merle's shoulder. His pulse calmed, the quiet night soothed him and the hours drew out.

Sleep's refuge released him slowly.

Presden turned onto his hip and let light through his lids. The curtains over the open window lifted gently in the breeze. Merle was lying beside him, her back to him, silent, motionless.

Then, as if she'd been waiting for him to wake, she turned over.

It wasn't Merle. Delphine was beside him, grown up and sober, regarding him.

Presden reached out. He touched her lower lip. It was moist. He took a lock of her hair between his fingers and felt it sliding through. I'm dreaming, he thought. But he wasn't sure.

"What are you thinking?" Delphine asked.

"Why have you come?"

Her eyes dulled, too hurt to reply.

"I'm losing my wife," he said.

"What is she to you?" his twin asked.

He searched her for envy or threat, but there was none. She peered at him with innocent eyes, the eyes of a child. "Why did you marry her?"

Presden shifted his head, as if to shake it.

"Please," she said.

He wanted to hide himself, but the boy inside him wouldn't deny her. He spoke slowly, describing Merle's strength, her energy, her courage, her child's spirit, her devotion to things that mattered.

"She's like me," Delphine guessed.

"Yes, she is."

"That's what you wanted?"

He nodded.

"She's afraid of me," his twin said. "Isn't she."

"She wants me to let go of you."

"Would you do that?" Delphine asked.

Her hand rose between them. Her fingers touched the scar on his chest.

"We're not done with each other," she said. "Are we?"

She spoke from her heart, and he answered from his.

"No," he said. "We aren't."

"What about Merle?" Delphine asked.

"I don't think it's—" He stopped himself.

"You don't think it's what?"

"—going to work out. She wants me to be someone I'm not."

Delphine made a simple face. "Who are you?"

He laughed. "Your brother."

She added her laughter to his. "I never wanted what Merle wants because I never grew up."

Delphine's arms were shorter. Her head had retracted—the pillow was no longer beneath it. She's shrinking, Presden thought. And so was he.

I never grew up. Her words stuck in his ear. A deeper meaning echoed inside him, but his mind couldn't grasp it. His chest was thinner, his legs shorter, his head smaller.

"Shall we be young again?" she murmured.

"We already are," Presden said. They were still shrinking, less than teens now.

"Smaller," she insisted, giggling.

Presden poked her middle and giggled back. "Eight's perfect for me."

"Me too," she said.

Delphine was so happy to have him back. His sister had lost her other half too. The Gator had stolen her future. Being young led away from dread and grief, and as they reached the eight year mark, the last of it slid away.

"No school," Delphine said.

"No school." He smiled, turning his head.

He could hear the sizzle of bacon downstairs. Delphine wrinkled her nose, sniffing the odors of coffee and gravy. He reached his hand under the pillow and drew the clock out. Delphine snatched it away. "No rules," she said, and she flung it across the room.

The spark in her eye lit all the fireworks hidden inside him. "We can do anything," he whispered.

She looked up. "Let's take the roof off."

As the words left her lips, the roof began to particulate. It crept and billowed like a rusty fog, and then the breeze caught its tags and ruffles, pulling it apart, carrying it away. The walls of the room were eroding as well, from the top down. They shrank to kid height, and then they were gone. The twins were still on the bed, but the bed was floating in a limitless sky, sunny and blue.

Delphine turned her head. "Can you hear them?"

At a distance, the trilling and piping sounded, and as Presden listened, the sound grew louder. "The Wish Terns," he said.

"There they are," Delphine cried.

The white vees of the Wish Terns appeared directly above them, darting and weaving through the luminous blue, piping their questions, frantic with curiosity, crazy to know.

"What's your wish?" Delphine asked.

"To be together forever," Presden replied.

"Here?"

He smiled.

"I have a better wish," she said. "Let's go back to where we started."

"The bayou?"

Delphine peaked her brows. "Mama."

"The house-on-stilts," he said softly, enjoying the idea.

She grabbed his shoulders. "No. Inside her."

"You mean—"

She tickled him. "Her tummy, Squeaky!"

"Is it fun in there?" Presden giggled.

"Don't you remember? It's like the lagoon. Better."

"It can't be better," he said.

"Well almost as good. And there aren't any gators."

The winds were mounting, blowing offshore. Harder they blew, harder and harder, lifting them into the air. The bed was gone. They were floating free now, with the Wish Terns flocking around them, weaving and squealing, wings like knives, red bills wide, eager to make their wish come true.

"Spread your arms," Delphine cried.

But he already had. And the winds were ready, buoying their bodies, gently, carefully, carrying them both.

They were gliding above the surf, the dike and the village behind them, the sea spread before them to the limit of sight. Its bubble nets wove, its combers foamed, and its rickracks flashed; and the magical sight washed every fear and sorrow away.

"They want to know something," Delphine said.

Presden listened closely. The Wish Terns had a language he understood.

"Are you wishing you'd never been born?" the birds asked.

"No. We just want Mama," he answered. "We want to be back inside her. Together."

"They were inside her?" one bird tittered. "Is that right, is that right?" others piped. "Sure, I remember. Oh I do too. We were there, we were there."

The birds seemed to be sorting it out.

"Before, before—that's the wish," they chattered. "Go

back, to go back. That's what they want? Is that what you want?"

"I think so." Presden looked at Delphine.

"That's it," she cried. "Take us back."

Without further ado, the Wish Terns put their red bills down, plunging as one, and the twins went with them. The hypnotic currents rippled below, chevrons thrumming, lozenges pulsing, fish mouths opening—

All together they crashed into the sea.

The water was warm. The bubbles swarmed, foam thick as cheese, fish mouths gaping as one. "Are you sure about this?" Presden muttered. Was Mama's tummy under the sea?

The terns were winging beside him, scything the water, piping madly. "Is she here? Maybe. What do you think?" Other birds seemed surer. "Oh yeah. I'm sure. Before they were born. I can remember. Me too. So can Presden."

"No I can't," he said.

The water was a frenzy of tern heads and claws and the elbows and tips of their flexing wings. "I remember them coming out," one piped. "Oh me too. Presden was sleeping. No he wasn't. He was frightened—to death. Well so was Delphine. You remember that? Yes, oh yes. I was scared too. The walls of the place were shaking. They were poking and jerking and kicking each other."

They were still heading down—Presden, Delphine, and the whole frenzied tribe of Wish Terns—deeper and deeper. And instead of growing colder, the sea grew warmer and thicker.

"No fun, no fun," a bird squealed. "So much pressure. You can't remember that. Sure I can. What were you doing? Watching, what about you? Pressure, too much pressure. That's how it's done. Really—how do you know? It isn't like breaking out of an egg. Oh, I remember now. Mama was clenching and clenching."

"We tried to grab hold of each other," Delphine said. She was remembering now.

"But the pressure pulled them apart," a bird piped.

"She squirmed away," another added.

"I did?" Delphine said.

"She did?" a tern echoed. "Yes," others answered, "she did, she did. She knew it was time. What's wrong with you? Can't you remember? She turned her back and put her head down."

"Delphine went first?" Presden said.

"Did Delphine go first?" birds squealed. "Yes, aren't you listening? Oh, I'm not surprised. Well neither am I. She was always in front. She was the leader."

"I was the leader sometimes," Presden objected.

Delphine huffed, "You know they're right."

"You came out crying," a tern recalled. "Did she? I don't remember that. I do—it was a victory cry. No, it was a cry of relief."

"The struggle was over," Delphine recalled. "But the light was blinding."

"The light, the light," the flock was tittering. "Her little hands—do you remember? I do. I do too. They were reaching. Groping. Delphine was confused. No she wasn't—she was reaching for him. You really think— Are you sure? What else would she be doing? She knew him so well— Did she? Come on, think about it. 'Where is my twin, where is my twin?'"

"I was behind," Presden guessed sourly.

"Not far, not far," a few birds reassured him. "Too much light. Too much, too much. Oh, that I remember. Do you? Oh yeah— Light, blinding light. But it was empty and cold. Presden was frightened," the terns piped as one.

"You can't remember that," he said.

"Yes we can, yes we can. She was gone. Then you reached out, and she was there."

The mob was still descending. The sea grew still thicker. Presden felt the warm currents barging against him. And then—they seemed to slow.

What's happening? he thought. Where are we? The descent was no longer plumb. They were angling, struggling for buoyancy.

"Look at yourself," a young tern yipped. "I can't see. Move aside— You're in the way. Oh dear— Can you believe—"

Presden peered at his arms. They were plump and stubby—the arms of an infant.

"We're almost there," a bird announced. "I don't remember this," another complained. "It's the hard part. This I remember. Don't be afraid, Presden."

"He's not afraid," Delphine said.

"It's narrower here," a Wish Tern warned. "Just a canal. The best way— You'll have to force yourself—"

"I know what a canal is," Presden said.

Stronger, thicker— The sea seemed to have walls that were pushing against him. They pushed and relaxed, pushed and relaxed; and at each push, the smothering walls stopped his breath. "Delphine?"

"It's tight in here," a tern piped. "Too tight, too tight," a half-dozen shrilled.

"Delphine?"

"There's not any room," she gasped.

They were all barely moving. "Keep going, keep going," the terns cried. "They're so close. How do you know? Was it really this hard? Don't stop now."

The crush was suddenly fierce. Presden felt something grip his chest and make his legs flail. His heart hammered, his head ached, the lines of current sunk into his flesh like razor threads.

"It's the same as then," an old tern lamented. "They're stuck. His shoulders won't go through. He didn't think he could do it. Can he? Maybe not. Don't stop, Presden."

All at once, the sea opened around him.

"You're nearly there," the Wish Terns piped.

The waters were sluggish now, barely moving. Presden could feel the thud of a distant tide. "That's it! Feel the pulse? The throbbing— You're back, you're back," the Wish Terns chattered. "That's your Mama's heart beating."

The womb was snug, but he had his place. Presden slid into it now, reaching, feeling. And there she was, suspended before him—the baby Delphine, lids closed, arms open. They were both so much smaller now, barely human—creatures you might find in a swamp and fish out with a net.

Their world was a watery one, a private lagoon, and they huddled and turned like amphibians in it, slick and sliding against each other.

The magic patterns were all around him. Strands of pearls ringed his arms, bubbles glittering, sliding as he shifted. Stars sprang from his toes and fingers. And his chest was lozenged, like a bed of mollusks showing their glowing interiors.

Delphine was penciled with colored threads, glowing lines that stitched her skin, entering and leaving, joining her body to the loom of the sea. The birthmark of magic, he thought. Patterns that would never fade or be forgotten.

He could feel her concentration. And then Delphine spoke.

Is it you? Is it really you?

Presden sighed and touched her, his heart crying out.

Where did you go? she said. *I've been here all this time, waiting.*

A tern choir rose, a sound of infinite longing broken into a hundred pieces.

You'll never be alone again, Presden promised. *I swear.*

One bird cooed, "Did you hear what he said?" Others chimed in, "She's happy, so happy. I didn't expect— They belong to each other. He's dreaming. Dreaming? I'm not so sure about that."

"The earth is no more," a misty bird piped. "There is only the sea. The struggle to be born—that was the dream."

Presden embraced his twin. Had the world beyond some-how ended? If not, in time he'd forget. He wished for that, hoping the Wish Terns could hear him.

Your warmth, your body, Delphine said. *The love I felt— I feel it again.*

And he felt her. Her relief, her welcome, her surprise, her joy. And when he touched her face, there were expressions to match. They were two—they had always been two—but it was as if they were one. The division—the distance, the sepa-ration— was finally gone.

An alarm was ringing.

Presden was splayed on the beach. He stirred as the surf pulled back in a whisper. The sea was reassuring him, leaving him with something stronger than faith.

Delphine lay on the sand beside him—a woman again, as he was a man. When he reached out to touch her, she turned to face him.

"You knew," she said, as the piping of the Wish Terns fad-ed. "You understood, before that night. You accepted the rule of the bayou. Whatever it gave us, you were willing. That was my brother's spirit."

"We belonged to the water," Presden said.

And then the dream was over, and he was alone on the bed.

He silenced the alarm, propped himself on an elbow, still dizzy, looking around. The loft, the inverted hull, a house on the dike— It all seemed unreal. The only clarity was inside him, deep inside, where he could feel Delphine and their private lagoon.

Presden pulled on fresh clothes and went looking for Merle.

Except for painting supplies and the half-built crib, the nursery was empty. He descended the stair and crossed the living room, wondering at the accidents of fate that had landed him there. Holland, he thought. A Dutch wife and a career as an engineer. When he entered the kitchen, he saw the back door was ajar.

Merle was sitting in the garden, facing the tomato trellis, the broken puppet across her knees. As he climbed the stone steps, she looked up. He could see the defeat in her eyes.

What could he tell her? She glanced at the puppet's face, and for a moment Presden felt how the puppet felt. The strings were tugging, but the sailor was battered and limbless. The show Merle had written couldn't go on.

"I love you," he said. "But—"

"You're going to leave me."

Presden shook his head. She didn't understand.

"You want me to destroy our son," she said.

Presden saw her dread and he felt it too. "No."

Merle's eyes clouded.

"I can't—"

"What?" she said. "Can't what? Be a father? What are you saying?"

"I'm not going to lose her."

Merle's chin rose. Her head tipped back and her eyes grew wider, as if she was finally seeing the canyon between them, so much larger than she'd ever imagined.

Presden returned to the living room and found his phone on the desk.

The Count answered on the second ring. "I'm listening," he said.

"Eight centuries is enough," Presden said. "The dike doesn't belong here."

Silence.

Presden imagined the Count in a dory on a stormy sea. His dark cape was wet, and his fedora was dripping. One eye glinted beneath the brim.

"I confess," the Count said, "I'm surprised."

"There's a time to defend, and a time to let go."

"I know how difficult this has been," the Count said.

No you don't, Presden thought.

"Well," the Count sighed, "the sea will be pleased."

Were the words wry? No, they were perfectly solemn.

For a moment, Presden wondered if the man had some idea what stirred in the hearts of those who belonged to water.

"We're ready to evacuate your neighbors," the Count said. "They'll have to be told that they're not coming back."

6

The gathering occurred in the weedy lot across from the swamped church.

Presden stood on a low rise with his hands at his sides. Being close to the water, the soil was woven with surf plants. Silvery sea holly raised prickly blooms at the edge of the rise. Beneath Presden's shoes, mats of rocket were crusted with salt. When he glanced at the crowd, they seemed to have settled, so he drew a long breath and began to speak.

As a result of the recent collapse, Presden said, his opinion had changed.

I'm on my own now, he thought. Merle had no interest in attending the announcement.

He'd briefed the Board, Presden went on, and they'd accepted his recommendation. The evacuation started that morning would be permanent.

Curses and groans crossed the lot. Jan kicked the weeds.

The Droomwater dike, Presden told them, would be destroyed, and the land it had protected would be given back to the sea.

"Just like that," a man said. "Sweep it all away."

"It's not too late," a woman protested.

They were all so afraid of the water. "The houses will be appraised and condemned." Presden avoided their eyes, speaking over their heads.

"When?"

"They're inspecting properties right now," he said.

The Count stood at the rear of the gathering wrapped in his cape, one arm hidden, watching. Presden looked past him toward the coast, imagining the big man understood. A fog was drifting toward them. *Sent from the water*, Presden thought. It muzzed the Count and filtered through the crowd, removing shoulders and blurring faces. Through the veil, Presden saw the Widow step forward, staff held high, an arthritic Moses trying to part the waters. "Take their money," she dared the others. Then she faced Presden. "I'm not going to leave."

Her rage didn't touch him. What did it matter?

The Count was moving through the crowd. He mounted the rise, stopped a few feet from Presden and began to speak.

The villagers' attention shifted. Presden closed his eyes and put his palms together. For the first time in many days, he was aware of his body. He could feel his leg muscles loosening, his blood circulating to the ends of his hands and feet, and flushing his cheeks.

The Count was fielding questions about the buyout, assuring people that they would be treated fairly. He had a deputy with him to review relocation and the demolition plan.

Presden glanced at the Count, and the Count paused to excuse him. Faces turned as Presden stepped down from the rise and found his way through the crowd. As he approached Jan and Fonelle, she bowed her head. Jan met his gaze.

"Maybe Droomwater Bay will be a good place to fish," Jan said.

Board officials spoke to each of the residents and gave them notice in writing. Movers and packers, the officials explained, were on their way. At 10 a.m. a video clip was sent to the residents of all the coastal villages. In it, the Count explained the sacrifice. "We've been fighting the sea for over a millennium," he said, "protecting our lands as best we can. Some of the protections were poorly conceived." He expressed his sorrow for the pain the decision would inflict on Droomwater. "But not every defense is a wise one. There are times when the better course is to yield."

At 11 a.m. the movers arrived with a convoy of vans and a platoon of packers, with orders to help the residents empty their homes by the end of the day. Every door was open, every yard and drive was piled with boxes. Pets were shuttled to a nearby town. Livestock was hauled to pens in the foothills. In a tent they erected in the weedy lot, a team of engineers organized the demolition.

At the end of the day, people left in their cars. Some had relatives or friends to stay with, but most headed for a school gymnasium inland, which would be used as an evacuation center.

The Widow Muldar had to be forcibly removed.

When a deputy and two officers paid her a visit, she locked herself in the attic. They had to slosh through the front room, climb the ladder and break down the door. They found her in her husband's clothes, cooking over a primus stove. She pretended she didn't see them, and when the deputy read her the order, she cut off an eel's head and threw it in a skillet. They took her into custody and led her away.

It didn't take long for the packers to box up Presden and Merle's belongings. They had little to say to each other. When the movers departed, Presden was standing on the dike, looking out to sea. A choice between sorrows. Now he'd made his. Were the waters content? Had they known how things would end, long in advance? What a person would give to see the future woven into those patterns.

When he returned to the house, the rooms were empty. He found Merle in the nursery, curled on the floor in a sleeping bag. He helped her into the bedroom. A thoughtful packer had left behind a pair of flats and a summer dress. Presden put them on her. He could feel her defeat, and a vain remorse rose inside him.

We shouldn't, he thought. But he joined her mourning and escorted her from room to room. Together, in silence, they said goodbye to their home.

It was a wistful goodbye, a litany of things that wouldn't occur. The rain wouldn't tap on the bathroom window. The berries wouldn't ripen beside the patio door. The leaves on the plane tree weren't going to turn. And the garden where Merle was going to sit with her child would never again see the sun.

When the litany ended, they passed through the front room into the entry. Presden's car was parked in the drive. There were photos of them on the entry wall.

"Why weren't these packed?" he wondered.

Merle regarded the images of the couple—posing, laughing, kissing.

"Who are they?" she said, as if the pictures were of strangers.

By the time the residents had left the village, charges had been planted along the dike's length and on either side of the plugged breach. It had begun to leak, and black streams were running between the houses.

Presden dropped Merle off at the evacuation center, and at the Count's insistence, he returned in a helicopter. It hovered over the half-submerged trawler, while a full round of explosives was lowered onto its deck. Then the chopper rose and all the charges were triggered at once. Presden viewed the destruction from overhead.

The air was filled with erupting peat and fragments of planking, and a roiling sea poured into the ragged gap.

Through the dark rain, Presden saw the flood enter the village, churning around the buildings closest. The Widow's house was knocked down. Two nearby were swamped and uprooted. The flood humped and frothed toward the church, boiling around homes on either side. The sea had been held back for centuries; now, with the gate open wide, it wasted no time.

In the distance, north and south of the village, the dike was like a line on a draftsman's drawing that was being erased. The line fuzzed and blurred, obscured by the rubbing waves.

The flood rose to the tops of Droomwater gardens and window sills. Houses trembled and shook, while the racing currents snaked between. The weaker buildings loosened and leaned. A few collapsed or were overturned. Through the chopper's tinted window, Presden saw the sea reach his home. The waters hooked, and a peat-stained maelstrom whirled around it, blackening the siding, punching through glass. The sight made him queasy, nauseous.

What was a home? he thought. Events, deep feelings, moments of decision, memories and hopes— You imagined all those grains added up to a firmament upon which you stood. But people were travelers. Time moved you through life. You dragged a tin can behind, trawling for whatever you could, significant or petty, catching everything but the water itself, which could never be caught.

The house seemed to sink. He mumbled a prayer that it would keep its footing, and it did. The walls remained straight while the ground floor was drowned. Where the front yard had been, the crown of the plane tree was a shaking bush. Then the black tide rose up the stone steps, and the garden and its tomato trellis disappeared.

The water level continued to rise, swollen like muscle at first, then spreading like mercury or silver lava, but with no steam or spray. The church nave was half-drowned, but the tower stood high above it. The demolition team had set a mic at the top, and through his headset Presden could hear the crush of dwellings and the crack of trees. An air horn began blowing bursts of threes.

Beneath the sounds of the demolition, he could hear the beat of the chopper blades like the crashing rhythm that had charmed their lives. The crashing was only a memory now. The dike was gone, and so were the battering waves.

The tides will be gentler, he thought. The sea, recognizing their sacrifice and acceptance, would bring peaceful currents and the desire to heal. He imagined that as the flood slid over the land, it would announce itself with scents of the bayou. The salt bite of oysters, the cypress perfume, the metallic odor of crabs and shrimp.

For him, the sea's incursion marked the end of denial, an admission that it was futile to ask his heart to forget. From here forward, somehow, he would live the watery life he'd shared with Delphine. Presden imagined the two of them on a tongue of water, passing into and through the flooded homes. The people were gone, but their dreams remained. His sister could hear them; and in time, he would too.

The pilot barked and pointed. There was something alive

on the roof of a house—a feral cat, wet and desperate. As they flew past, the cat's eyes followed Presden.

He kept his promise to Merle. They met in the parking lot of the ultrasound clinic.

Despite her upset, there was care in her eyes. Presden opened his arms and they held each other, rocking in the backwash of memory.

"Someday," Merle said. "Someday—"

She peered into his eyes.

He waited, letting her speak.

"—you'll wish you'd made a different decision."

"Maybe I will," he said. He looked down.

There was a small bulge in Merle's middle. Her womb was a secret place, and he was about to see inside it. His dream of the mystery of life's beginning was very much with him.

The clinic staff was brisk and professional, but their clients gave the proceedings a party atmosphere. Expectant parents, friends and relations filled the halls with surprise and celebration. That made it harder for Merle and Presden. Neither could put on a cheerful face. When their turn came, a clinician escorted them into a small white room.

Short and plump, with a prying smile, her manner was chirpy at first. But she'd quickly sensed that for them the procedure would be a more sober affair. After a brief preamble, Merle removed her clothing and put on a cotton gown.

"Are you comfortable?" the clinician asked.

Merle nodded. She was lying with her back on the table.

"And how about you?" The clinician dimmed the lights, turned back to her monitor and checked the settings.

"I'm fine," Presden said. He was seated on a chair a few feet away.

"Alright." The clinician leaned over Merle, parted the gown and squirted gel from a tube onto Merle's belly.

Then she raised the scanning probe in her gloved hand.

Presden imagined himself at dusk, sitting on the shore of Droomwater Bay with the breeze in his face, west glow fading. He was eating tuna from a can with his fingers, sharing a piece with the cat beside him, thinking of sleep and the descent into dream.

The clinician lowered the scanning probe onto Merle's middle.

Light splashed across the dark screen. Blue jags, blue ripples.

"Here is our amniotic fluid," the clinician said. "We measure the quantity. It's important to fetal well-being."

"And here—" She tapped on her keyboard with her left hand and moved the probe with her right. "—is the baby's chest."

Presden searched the screen.

"At the bottom?" Merle asked.

"Here's the spine," the clinician pointed. "And here is the heart." She glanced at Merle. "Can you see it beating? Listen—"

A sound like a flexing saw came from speakers nearby.

"The heart rate is normal," the clinician said. "Everything looks and sounds fine. Can you see your child?"

"I can't," Merle said.

"Neither can I," Presden murmured.

The screen filled with blue splashes as the clinician turned the probe.

Presden heard whispering at a distance. He needed sleep badly. He leaned forward, trying to focus. All he could see on the screen was a mass of floating rhomboids. As he watched, they bumped and pulsed. Then the screen's center blacked, like a cod's eye rimmed with silver, seeing a fantastical world.

"Raise your right hip. Just a little."

The clinician leaned closer, edging the probe across Merle's belly.

Presden strained to see. The air seemed wet and salty. Ranks of rickracks patterned the glass, crossing the screen like a curtain being drawn. A curled shape appeared. Was that the child?

"There we are," the clinician said. "Let's get a photo. You can take it home with you. There's the forehead, the lips and chin." She pointed. "Here is a leg. We want to be sure that the bones are straight and the proper length. They look perfectly normal."

Merle sighed.

The clinician squinted at the screen and shifted the probe. "Wait a minute." She pushed on Merle's abdomen. "Well," she laughed. "It looks like there might be two in there."

Presden's heart stopped. The screen image froze. His great longing, his desperate need— It congealed suddenly into something real. He and his twin had returned to life—inside Merle.

"Are there twins in your family?" the clinician asked.

"No." Merle stared at him, stunned. "My husband was a twin."

"That wouldn't matter," the clinician said.

Presden saw a small arm on the screen. It flexed and straightened, like Delphine's when they swam in the lagoon.

"Oop. My mistake," the clinician said. "It was a shadow. There's only one." She pushed Merle's belly again and shifted the probe. "Congratulations," she smiled, sitting back in her chair. "It's a baby girl."

Snores and murmurs echoed in the crowded gymnasium. The lights were off, except for a pair of sconces by the washroom doors. The Droomwater villagers were on the floor, as intimate as they'd ever been with each other, lying on futons, wrapped in blankets, bundled in sleeping bags. Presden was at the crowd's edge on a mattress, alone, on his side.

He was deep in dream.

The place he was in was close and warm, soft and watery. Presden was floating, cradled by chevrons, penciled with lines that had woven, zigzag and iridescent, through his sensitive flesh, while silver-blue rhomboids pulsed around him.

His arms were stubby and so were his legs. Waves lulled and rocked him, and his thoughts of Delphine did the same, as if the time between his dreams of her were merely the distance, the oscillation, between one wave and the next.

She had been with him for as long as he could remember, and she had always been close, her shadowy figure suspended, pale and naked, within arm's reach. They were fetal mates, ultrasound twins, with the sea's soothing throb kneading their hearts and the rickrack currents threading their skin. In the warmth and darkness, they were more than two creatures struggling toward life. The sea made them more.

They could taste the sea, and the taste was salty, teeming with scents. They could smell the brine and blood of alien creatures. They could hear—not just with their ears, but with their bodies—the tidal drumming, the foamy hiss, bubbles wriggling up, and the clamor of impossible voices. And the sea filled their minds, as well, with impossible images.

Delphine's arm extended. He could feel her hand through layers of membrane. He did the same, touching her leg. It was soft and pliant. Delphine's chest touched his, and then they were holding each other, cradling and rocking in each other's arms, lost in the reverie of the magical sea.

"We cared for each other," she said, "in the swamps and lagoons. And here too, before we entered the world."

I'm dreaming, he thought.

"Dreaming," she echoed. "We've spent an eternity here, holding each other, curled together, listening to the rhythm of Mama's heart."

Water creatures, he thought.

"Water creatures," she said. "Sleeping together, waking together, sensing everything sharply and truly."

Her lips opened and closed, breathing the sea. Her arms still held him, but her face turned away.

"Children cry in the womb," Delphine said.

Her voice was hushed.

"I have heard you cry," she said.

He could feel her reluctance to say any more.

"Things are going to happen to us," she said, "once we're born. Sad things."

I can't lose you, he thought.

Delphine touched his cheek.

I deserve you, he told her.

"Of course you do."

It was as if their words had been overheard. A chorus of voices sounded, muted and smothered, like a recording playing inside a closed trunk.

"Who will decide?" the voices sang. "Who will decide?"

The close place, lulling and warm, was expanding. The walls grew rugged, mottled and crusty, and shelved with silt.

Delphine's eyes looked larger, her lips and her brow—Her hand left his cheek, and as her arm unfolded, it was larger too. Her trunk grew longer and so did her legs. Presden remembered the sack on the sea floor and how he'd discovered her. She was growing now, as she'd grown then. And he was growing with her.

"Who will decide?" the choir warbled.

Sheets of sand rippled past, born by the currents, the drapes of time once again dividing. The Oyster Sisters, shells open wide, were perched on their shelf, lustrous mouths brightening the dim chamber. As Presden looked toward them, a current gushed between him and his sister, hurling them apart.

Into the gap, a rocky stage lifted, and on it were the four magisters and Big Oyster settled in his commodious shell.

Presden was full-grown now, and his twin was too. They stood gazing at each other while the chorus faded.

Magister Titus crinkled his lip, consulting his docket. "Does Presden Deserve Delphine?"

Presden faced the bench.

"The question is before the court," Magister Flabus said.

"Do you deserve your sister," Magister Titus explained. "Was your devotion sufficient."

"It was absolute," Presden said. "If you had any idea—"

"Yes, yes," Big Oyster smoothed his robe. "We've been watching."

"He loved her truly," the Sisters sang. "We were mistaken."

"I agree with the girls," Magister Right opined. "Not guilty."

Magister Flabus raised himself, his belly slopping over his bill. "Not guilty."

"He's a selfish bastard," Magister Curlis said, "but I concur."

"Selfish and cruel," Magister Titus said darkly. "His marriage to Merle has to count against him. And now— He's abandoning her and their unborn child."

"It's wrong, I know," Presden said. He looked at Delphine.

He thought she might speak in his defense, but she had pursed her lips.

"He loves Delphine," a row of cocktail oysters cried.

"He's given up everything for her," Magister Right pointed out.

"Love is always the excuse," Magister Titus objected.

"True," Big Oyster said. "But it's the best one." He flapped his mantle, dismissing the dissenting vote. "The court has reached a decision." He clacked his top shell. "Not guilty," he pronounced. "You do indeed deserve your twin."

The Oyster Sisters burst into song, rocked in unison by a wayward current.

Presden turned and embraced his sister. "It's all working out."

"All right," Big Oyster said. "It's time for you to leave."

Presden glanced at the judge. Who was he speaking to? When he looked at Delphine, there was remorse in her eyes. Her lips were trembling.

"We're going to spend forever together," Presden said, clasping her, holding her close.

Big Oyster filtered the situation. "You may have made some incorrect assumptions."

The chamber was silent. Even the Sisters were mute.

"We settle troubles of the heart here," Big Oyster said. "We don't have the power to bring the dead back to life."

A long shadow entered the chamber. When Presden looked up, he saw the silhouette of the Gator.

"Who do I have to talk to?" he insisted.

Big Oyster's lid twitched. A string of bubbles rose from his lips. "If you find him, we'll all be very impressed."

Presden faced his sister. "We're not done with each other," he echoed her words.

"I can't stay with you."

"You're here with me now," he objected.

"It's only a dream," she said. "And this is the last."

With that, the chamber was filled with sighs.

"In our place of miracles," Delphine said, "there's an innocent child. As helpless as we were. But she's alive."

A sob burst from Presden's chest. He reached out, stumbling toward his sister. "Why have you done this?"

"You would never have let go of me," Delphine said. "I know my brother."

Presden hugged his twin, shaking with sobs. The chamber was silent.

"A very sad case," Big Oyster murmured. "My dear fellow, if it's any consolation, this is all inside you."

Then his aged hinge creaked, and the wrinkled shell closed. The other oysters were closing too. The nacreous mosaic faded, the light in the cave dimmed, and the rocky stage began to descend.

Presden hugged his twin with all his strength, refusing to let her go. But it wasn't enough. She slipped through his arms, sinking into the darkness, following the oysters into the deep.

Come back, he cried. *Please come back.*

Her body dwindled and fogged. Beneath her, the darkness was spiraling like a well; and Delphine—all pale and wispy—was vanishing into it.

Deep in the spiral he saw a child's eyes, glinting like they did when she had something wicked in mind. Then the wicked look turned into a knowing one, misty with sorrow, swollen with love and thwarted devotion.

And then she was gone.

Presden woke in the noisy gymnasium. He'd been in a distant place, it seemed. And the journey back was a long one.

He lifted himself, looking around as he tightened his belt and buttoned his shirt. Evacuees were rising, lining up by the washroom doors and the breakfast tables. Presden combed his hair with his fingers and turned to scout the crowd.

His wife was seated on a cot by the referee's table. He started toward her.

Merle saw him coming and turned her head.

Presden knelt beside her. "Are you hungry?" When she said no, he touched her chin, looked in her eyes and asked if she would walk with him.

They passed through the gymnasium doors in silence. School was in session and the voices of children reached them from classrooms and playground. The path branched and they followed it, winding through a glade and a garden.

"How is she this morning?"

"Busy," Merle said.

He reached into his shirt pocket and removed the ultrasound photo.

They examined it together.

"I'm sorry—" He slowed his steps.

So much had been said. So many raw and misguided emotions— And so much pain.

"You're a wonderful woman. You've been a wonderful wife. But you were wrong about being lucky. You haven't been."

She looked away.

"The man you married brought his bad fortune with him. I wanted to protect you," he said. "But I couldn't."

She didn't reply.

"The dreams have ended," Presden said.

"Ended?" Merle squinted. How could he know that?

"She's returned to the dead," he said.

"You're not making sense."

"She didn't come for me," he tried to explain. "She was here for us."

Merle turned to face him, sun glinting the points of her fishhooked hair.

"Our family. Our child. Our future," he said.

"Have things changed?"

As softly and humbly as he could, he said, "They have."

Merle halted, and he did too.

"Bringing our little girl into the world—" He sounded so tentative, he might have been asking a question.

She took the photo from him, eyeing it as if it was some kind of puzzle.

"I wasn't dreaming the dead had come back to life." Presden touched the photo. "I was dreaming of this."

Merle's chin fell. Her shoulders sagged, and she gasped as if struck.

Presden heard her sob, and when he reached out, she poured into his arms.

No words, she was frail and shaking. As strong as she was, she seemed light as a bird.

"I love you," he swore. "Both of you."

Merle shuddered. Then her spine straightened, and the mistrust she'd borne—unwelcome, unnatural—saw its error, and he felt all that was her coming back to him.

She would never understand the depth of his loss—that couldn't be shared. But she could know that his future belonged to her.

She put her hands on his loins and pulled him closer, pressing her belly to his. He felt the baby move, and he heard Merle's thought: *This is what we've created.*

"A perfect girl in a perfect life." She spoke gently, as if recanting. "As perfect as we can make it."

"I promise: there will always be love around her."

His wife took his words, Presden knew, as a pledge of constancy to her and their child, and that's how he meant it. But he was thinking, as well, of Delphine and the sea.

His old world, protected, contained, had been drowned; and a new world was in its place—a world in which one he loved might be taken from him, but from which love itself could never be erased.

That afternoon the Count arrived with a half-dozen lawyers and accountants. One carried a boxful of envelopes into the gymnasium. An attorney spread confections on the referee's table, while the accountants handed out the assessments. Some of the villagers seemed at loose ends, stunned or confused. But many brightened when they saw the property appraisals. One stood with the letter in his hand, waving it under his chin, as if the breeze was restoring him. Where would they live? Into what new adventure would the change thrust them? The Widow sat on a folding chair in a corner by herself; but for everyone else, the end of the village wasn't a deathblow. The children were happy enough eating muffins and using the lines on the gymnasium floor for a game of hop-on-one-foot.

The Count handed the last envelope to Merle. "Thank you," he said. He glanced at Presden. "A difficult matter. But things will work out."

With no more than that, the big man bowed and stepped away.

Presden watched him move through the crowd, listening, shaking hands, offering words of encouragement.

"I loved that house." Merle eyed the envelope. "I really did."

He took it from her, folded it and put it in his pocket. "Shipworms will enjoy the picnic table."

Merle nodded.

"There will be cod in our bedroom," he said. "And shrimp in the garden."

"Barnacles on the fridge," she sighed, "and starfish in the sink." It helped her to say it out loud.

"I've been thinking about where we might live," he said, "the three of us."

Presden reached for her hand and knitted his fingers through hers.

The year following the demolition, the stubs of the Droomwater dike eroded. They were slumping and dangerous places. But on a few smooth stretches, couples or families might be seen on clear days, playing catch on the grass or relaxing in lounge chairs. As they'd planned, Presden and Merle, and their little girl, spent an afternoon there. Merle took a photo of her taking wobbly steps on the tumbled peat.

Presden taped the photo on a blank page at the end of the Storybook. Beneath it, he wrote, "Delphine and Dad on her first birthday."

As the years advanced, the embayment changed. At low tide, boaters could see rooftops beneath the surface. It seemed like the ghost of the village came and went. But at each retreat, the sea took pieces of the worm-eaten dwellings down to the deep. Observers marked a steady deterioration—the peaks of crumbling gables, the ribs of leaning walls. By the fifth year most of the village was gone. Only the church tower remained. At the same time, the native wildness of the coast returned. The verge was lush and teemed with birds, and the coastal current, slowing and turning, brought schools of fish. Golden sands aproned one side of the tower's base; on the other, oysters colonized its bricks.

At the visitor center, they rented a dory. Presden rowed. As they neared the tower, the terns nesting on its golden shore rose in a cloud, weaving and piping over them. Presden feathered the oars and pulled them out. Merle removed the cake from a box, set it on the thwart and lit the candles.

"Eight's a lucky number," she said.

Presden kissed his daughter's cheek. "Make a wish."

Delphine closed her eyes.

After the celebration, they went swimming together. Like her parents, the child had a natural comfort with water.

Rich Shapero's novels dare readers with giant metaphors, magnificent obsessions and potent ideas. His casts of idealistic lovers, laboring miners, and rebellious artists all rate ideas as paramount, more important than life itself. They traverse wild landscapes and visionary realms, imagining gods who in turn imagine them. Like the seekers themselves, readers grapple with revealing truths about human potential. *Dreams of Delphine* and his previous titles—*The Slide That Buried Rightful, Dissolve, Island Fruit Remedy, Balcony of Fog, Rin, Tongue and Dorner, Arms from the Sea, The Hope We Seek, Too Far,* and *Wild Animus*—are available in hardcover and as ebooks. They also combine music, visual art, animation and video in the TooFar Media app. Shapero spins provocative stories for the eyes, ears, and imagination.